TALES
from the
JANITOR

TALES from the JANITOR

FROM DUSTING DESKS TO BUSINESS SUCCESS

CHARLES STROBEL

ILLUSTRATIONS BY AMANDA ZUNDEL

STROB PRESS
Greensburg, PA

> For orders or additional information go to
> www.fromthejanitor.com

© 2009 Charles Strobel

All rights reserved. No part of this book may be reproduced or transmitted in any form or by any means, electronic or mechanical, including photocopying, recording, or by any information storage and retrieval system, without permission in writing from the publisher.

Published by
STROB Press
Greensburg, PA
www.fromthejanitor.com

Publisher's Cataloging-in-Publication Data
Strobel, Charles.

    Tales from the janitor : from dusting desks to business success / written by Charles Strobel ; illustrated by Amanda Zundel. — Greensburg, PA : STROB Press, 2009.

    p. ; cm.

    ISBN13: 978-0-9841545-0-0

    1. Building cleaning industry—Management. 2. Building cleaning industry—Anecdotes. 3. Success in business. I. Zundel, Amanda. II. Title.

HD9999.B882 S77 2009
648.5068-dc22   2009907736

Project coordination by Jenkins Group, Inc.
www.BookPublishing.com

FIRST EDITION

Cover design by Chris Rhoads
Interior design by Brooke Camfield
Illustrations by Amanda Zundel

Printed in the United States of America

13 12 11 10 09 • 5 4 3 2 1

Dedication

To all the wonderful people who built the business. I am ever so thankful for the effort, dedication, and creativity without which it would not have been possible to build a great business. Some of those great people still work at the company, some have retired, some have moved away, and some have passed away. All are missed!

Contents

Foreword	xi
Acknowledgments	xiii
Introduction	xv
Part I Developing the Aptitude and Capability to Create a Successful Business	**1**
Chapter 1: The Road to Success	**3**
College and Chemistry	5
Graduation Dilemma	7
Business Lessons at the Beach	9
Teaching and Business	12
Lessons from the Navy	19
The McDonald's Lesson	26
Who Gets the Worm?	28
Camp Director	32
Part II The Illustrative and Anecdotal Stories about What Janitors See and Hear	**35**
Chapter 2: Sex in the Cleaning Business	**37**
Short Skirts and Long Legs	39
That Service Is Not in Your Specifications	42
Has Anyone Seen This Butt?	44

Wet Mop across the Face	46
Four-Wife Rotation System	48
Sunday at the Office	50
The Morning After	52
Service with a Show	54
Factory Fashions	56
Chapter 3: Great People	**59**
Janitor with the PhD	61
The "Ace" in a Walker	64
The Ugly Duckling	67
Big Bag of Money!	71
Surprising Talent	72
Part-Time People Deserve Benefits	74
Ask and You Shall Receive	78
Four Old Fellows	80
No-Cost Training	83
Chapter 4: Hard to Believe . . . But True	**87**
Workplace Tobacco	89
All the Crackers You Can Eat	91
The Thundering Herd	93
Raising the Dead	95
Tasty Legal Fees	98
Speed Bumps in the Road of Progress	101
What Driver's License?	103
A Moment of Silent Prayer	105
I Wouldn't Hire You on a Bet	107
Learning to Read	109
Simple Things	111
Lawyer Meltdown	113
Luck	116

Chapter 5: Government Is Here to Help — 121
- An Al Capone Imitation — 123
- I Owe How Much? — 125
- You Are Not Employees Anymore — 128
- Three Philadelphia Lawyers — 133
- We Found a New Job for You — 138
- The Roads Are Closed — 140
- OSHA Wants What? — 141
- Nonprofit — 143
- Common Sense — 147

Chapter 6: Management—Good, Bad, and Ugly — 149
- Not Me! Where Can I Hide? — 151
- Opportunity Knocks — 157
- Gestapo Mentality — 159
- Cutting Rags for Workers' Compensation — 161
- Never Believe a Salesperson — 165
- Machiavelli Would Be Proud — 167
- A Learning Experience for Kids — 169
- Mafia — 172
- Quality versus Luxury — 175
- Sometimes It Is Good to Be Naive — 178
- The Truth — 180
- Creative Thinking — 182

Epilogue — 187

About the Author — 191

For Orders or Additional Information — 192

Foreword

As a businessman and longtime happy customer of Chuck Strobel's janitorial company, I got to know him both as a private person and as a businessman. I am both honored and delighted to write the foreword for this exciting book.

Tales from the Janitor is an inimitable collection of both erudite and entertaining stories about people whom Chuck Strobel encountered on his long and winding road to become a millionaire janitor. In his quest for wealth, he saw good, and he saw bad, but always he saw raw human nature in motion.

Starting from the early time when he and his loyal and partnering wife were the only employees in their start-up company to the time the company had grown to nearly five hundred people, he passionately grew to be a senior executive in a successful janitorial company. Here he became burdened with the complex issues and the endless stream of problems, disappointments, and challenges that typically face a CEO of a much larger company. Moreover, he was without the levels of management support that a larger company has. To add to the maze of problems that comes with any business, the janitorial business has the distinction of typically employing many part-time people and having a larger turnover of employees than most businesses.

There were days when scheduling five hundred people to report timely to as many as a hundred different cleaning destinations was one of the most difficult challenges. Yet, his foresight, propelled by his relentless tenacity to succeed, inched him to the day when he sold his company to become a millionaire. In the ensuing chapters, in an earnest and often jocular way, he talks openly about his problems and his successes and the people who made them happen. How he successfully handled these challenges is in this book and can be applied to any business.

Although this book is a must-read for young entrepreneurs, equally it is a read for everyone in terms of heartfelt stories that reflect a stirring level to which common people can rise, a static level at which many sadly remain, and a state of welfare to which the more unfortunate fall. There are stories that will leave you shaking your head in shocking disbelief. There are stories that will make you laugh or even cry. And in some stories you will even see yourself. That you are entertained is without uncertainty. That you miss reading this book is without fortune.

A customer of many years,
Robert Koveleskie

Acknowledgments

Writing this first book took far more time and effort than I thought it would. An accomplished author, Don Aslett, produced a book titled *How to Write & Sell Your First Book*. Without the guidance and instruction contained in that book, this poor effort of mine would not have been possible.

Those people who know of my remarkable talent to misspell so much of the English language in such creative and mystifying arrangements of letters will forever be thankful to those who edited and corrected this collection of stories. My thanks to Robert and Judith Koveleski, James Liddle, Dave Samuel, and James Harrold for their efforts in making so many corrections.

Amanda Zundel is a talented young artist who produced the artwork for this book—while making plans for her own wedding. That has to be dedication to completing a project.

My wife, Lyn, endured my writing this book over a couple of years while we were supposed to be on vacation. I always seemed to be too busy when we were not away on a vacation. She also made the initial corrections on the early rough drafts before I dared to let anyone else see them.

Introduction

Tales from the Janitor is fact, not fiction. It is a series of separate stories about people and events I encountered in the course of becoming a professional janitor and growing a very successful business. This is not strictly a business book; it is also an entertainment book told from an autobiographical perspective. However, the tales from the janitors provide excellent tutoring for all those who would entertain the thought of owning their own successful business. I assure you that if you learn the lessons from this collection of tales, you will be successful in all your endeavors.

The initial chapter describes some of the events, lessons, and education that contributed to the molding of an individual with the aptitude and capability to produce a great company from nothing. The next chapters have a series of short stories about the people and the customers I encountered while performing my janitorial duties. The chapters are arranged by general topics to help you focus on the stories that you find most entertaining. I suspect that many of you have wondered about what janitors actually see and hear. Rest assured that janitors see and hear almost everything, and now you can read about those illustrative, anecdotal episodes. *Every incident described herein actually happened.* The people are real, and only some of the names have been changed, where I believed it was necessary to protect the guilty and to avoid lawsuits. Where the people did great things, be assured those names are accurate.

Many of the stories are from a time when the janitorial service company was still very new. That was a time when I had more personal contact with the cleaning staff as well as greater day-to-day contact with our customers. By the time the company had grown to close to five hundred people I had become senior executive with all the issues and challenges that any CEO of a large company faces, but I always missed the more personal contact of the smaller company.

The stories are intended to be entertaining. I hope that you will find great examples of human nature and even see yourself in many of the separate stories or recall similar incidents in your own life. Some of these stories will reflect the greatness to which people rise, while other stories will leave you shaking your head in disbelief. Sometimes you'll cry, and sometimes you'll laugh, but you should always find the tales entertaining. I am most confident that you will find that truth can be as entertaining as fiction.

Part I

Developing the Aptitude and Capability to Create a Successful Business

The stories in the first chapter of this book deal with some of the life experiences that molded me and provided some of the lessons that were to become so important in creating a very successful business. As you read the different stories in this first chapter, it may be fun to realize how much of the narrative would also apply to you. The stories are not in chronological order, as in a biography, because many of the stories would have overlapping time frames and the book is not a biography. The stories are about lessons learned through life's experiences and how those lessons can be applied to the creation and operation of a successful business.

This first chapter deals with some personal learning experiences, while the remaining chapters in Part 2 of *Tales from the Janitor* are the entertaining anecdotal stories as experienced by the janitorial staff. Those stories or tales provide you with an interpretive opportunity to see many of the business lessons from Chapter 1 being applied by the janitors who just might be smarter than a great many politicians and business executives.

Chapter 1:
The Road to Success

College and Chemistry

Reality struck like a bolt of lightning.

In the sixties when I was getting out of college, I believe choosing the right career was more important to me than it would be today. Back then, the husband was expected to be the breadwinner. Today, that responsibility is shared more and more by both spouses.

A typical college student, I spent a lot of time thinking about a career. I thought of going into medicine. That was one of the reasons I was majoring in chemistry. Doctors are paid well, and it's a respectable and giving profession. But I decided against it because I didn't like the idea of spending at least four more years in school, along with an internship, hospital rotations, and residency. And besides, I didn't have the money that it would take. I began to look at other opportunities.

Being a chemist sounded like a good idea for a career. But an interview for a summer job with a Fortune 500 company changed my mind. Until the very end, the interview went well. Grades, awards, and part-time jobs were all worked into the discussions, and I did my best to be charming and ever-so agreeable. I thought I had it locked when the gentleman interviewing me asked what I could do for his company. Now, anyone who has ever worked in sales knows such a question was an apparent "buy signal." It looked like that summer job would be mine, and I thought I would ice it with a creative reply to his question. Trying to be as unpretentious as possible, I said something like, "The experience of working at such an important research laboratory is far more important than what I would actually be doing, and I would be pleased if you merely wanted me to wash test tubes." He paused and, with a slight dismissive undertone in his gruff voice, grumbled, "Well, now, that is what we use the guys with the BS degrees for." The books I had read on having a good interview didn't cover this. I pressed my perspiring hand forward on the chair arm and made myself slightly taller in the chair as I gestured with a raised eyebrow and a smile to signal that I understood that he was just having fun with me. But I was looking into a poker face that was telling me he was serious and my prospect for this summer job was in trouble.

On the drive back to my college, I had time to reflect on the interview. As a chemist, what type of work would I really be doing? Then, reality struck like a bolt of lightning.

The only interesting work in the field of chemistry was going to be done by the guys with the PhDs—and graduate school was out of reach for me. It meant tuition and expenses for three more years of school. It was money I didn't have and didn't want to borrow. Even if I was hired as a chemist, without a PhD it was clear that I could be stuck in endlessly boring tasks. A picture flashed in my mind of washing test tubes and doing the percent of iron determinations in samples for years at a time. That was not a pretty picture. What to do now?

Graduation Dilemma

Work accomplished is inversely proportional to the time available to accomplish it.

There was an even bigger potential dilemma for young college students graduating in the mid-sixties. Vietnam was becoming a major conflict. There was a real possibility of being drafted and sent to some rice paddy to shoot at people. I certainly did not like the idea of shooting at people and thought even less of them shooting at me. I did not want to get drafted and did not want to spend the time and money on that PhD. This was a real predicament. Like so many other young men, I had to chart a postgraduation course of action. So, now the overwhelming question was, What to do? The solution I found was to apply for the Navy's Officer Candidate School. Big ships seemed much safer, and perhaps I would get to see some of the world, as advertised in the recruiting slogan "Join the Navy and see the world." Apparently, lots of people had the same idea because the program was exceptionally competitive.

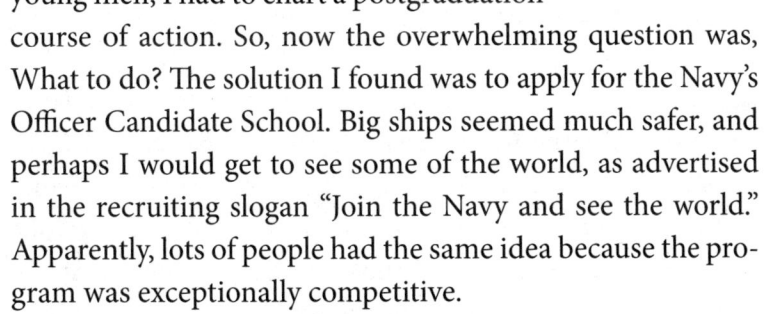

The Navy considered that I was active in the university's student government as a student legislative representative, dorm president, and resident men's association president. I was also a supervisor for several student work crews, and while in college I also held several part-time jobs to earn the money to pay for my schooling. My summer job as the program director of a large Boy Scout summer camp, with a significant staff under my direction, was also a large plus in the leadership qualities the Navy was looking for. However, I had considerable concerns about getting the appointment because my grade point average was well below that of my competitors for those appointments.

After my first two years at college, I found myself on academic probation, with a cumulative GPA of 1.99. After that scare, I got serious and turned in 3.7 to 4.0 semesters. The Navy looked at the last two years and excused the earlier grades. They apparently assumed that I just grew up.

The interesting thing is that the improvement did not come about solely because of the scare or some mysterious maturity. The academic improvement was really driven by something very different. My academic probation had dumped upon me nearly continuous lecturing from my well-meaning parents. I responded by paying for all my college, so I could nicely tell them to "get off my case."

A strange thing happened as I put together a series of jobs. The more part-time jobs I had, the better my grades became. I had also become much more involved in many different school activities, which took even more time. The GPA seemed inversely proportional to the time available to work on the academics. This was the first example of what I would come to recognize as a well-known business axiom. It states simply: "The work accomplished is inversely proportional to the time available to accomplish it." Necessity had forced me to become very efficient with the little remaining time that was available for academics. That was a really great lesson for a future business and for life in general. There is also a corollary for that axiom. It says, "If you need something done, give it to a busy man."

Business Lessons at the Beach

*They do so because they like you
and they like the way you treat them.*

The Navy gave me an appointment to the Officer Candidate School for a start in February, the year after my June graduation. After graduating, I thought a little R & R was in order, so I went to Ocean City, Maryland, with three graduating friends. I did not have to earn enough money for the next year's college expenses, as in past years. It was a nice situation to be in. It really did not matter how much money I made, as long as my expenses were covered until I became Navy property. My friends and I were sitting on the beach and were enjoying the sun and the surf, and also "babe-scoping" the beach scenery, when I decided that I should get a job and stay in the resort town for the summer.

My friends laughed at the thought of getting a job and a place to stay in the few hours left before the driver was to leave for home. Because we had driven to the beach for the day, I had only a bathing suit, shorts, a T-shirt, and sneakers. The first stop was a cheap clothing store for long pants, a golf shirt, and the cheapest shoes I could find. An hour and a half later, I had a job at a beachfront motel, where I was to be a waiter. The motel provided a room and two meals a day.

The new waiter job started at 5:00 a.m. and was over, on most days, by 1:30 in the afternoon. This left the afternoon open for beach time, with party time in the evening. The beachfront motel restaurant had a fair crowd in the very early morning, from the fishermen, followed by the sunrise beachcombers. Next came the families with younger kids, followed by the young adult crowd in the late morning. The families, who went to the beach at nine in the morning, were back for lunch well before noon, and the restaurant was dead by one thirty in the afternoon. The evening was also very quiet; people either went to the boardwalk or went out to better restaurants.

An elderly lady owned the motel. She provided some important lessons on how to really irritate customers. She inherited the motel a few years before, and her business had been steadily dropping year by year. She blamed everyone and everything except herself. The poor lady never had a friendly word for anyone. Her demeanor was definitely not the friendly McDonald's smile with the "How can I help you?" attitude. She so alienated customers that they confided to us members of the staff that they would not be back next year.

There was plenty of "feedback," but still she was unable to see herself as the principal reason for the continued downward trend of her business. She could not keep the business that she had, and she certainly was incapable of growing more business. Years later, as my own business grew, I used examples of her egregious behavior at management meetings. We had some laughs, and it helped to drive home the attitudes that any competitive business must have. The big lesson to be learned was that customers do not have to use your product or service. *They do so because they like you and they like the way you treat them.*

I suspect that you are now thinking that I am wrong and that the real key is having a great product or service. Yes, your product or service must be up to the necessary standards. However, that is only the price of entry to the field of play. If you actually have a superior product, you still will not do well if you do not treat customers well. *People do business with you or your company because they like you and they like the way you treat them.* It really is that simple!

Customers, or prospective customers, justify their decisions any way they need to. Later, when I looked back, it seemed strange that I had learned so much about a service business without even knowing what I was learning. I am still amazed at how important that learning was to become when I did start my own service company, which was still more than a few years in the future.

FROM DUSTING DESKS TO BUSINESS SUCCESS   11

Teaching and Business

*You stimulate enthusiasm, and
that enthusiasm becomes contagious.*

After a really great summer with my beach resort job, I returned to my parents' home in late September. I believed that it would be easy to find a job until I reported to the Navy in early February. It took only two days to realize that finding a job was not going to be easy. This was 1965, and almost always the first question posed in any interview was "What is your draft status?" or "May I see your draft card?" Because my card indicated that I had already been selected "to report," no employer wanted to waste his or her time. The typical response was "You seem like a good prospect for our company. Call us when you get back." Clearly, the standard job approach was not going to work.

My brother was a senior at the local high school, and I learned through him that the school was desperately short of substitute teachers. The school was putting five or six classes together in the auditorium just to get through the day. I thought that if the school was that hard up, it might not be so concerned that I would be Navy property in a few months. If I managed to work just a couple days a week, I would get by until then.

One bright Thursday morning I went to the school and explained to an administrator why I was there. She listened with obvious excitement and asked me to wait while she got the vice principal. My people-reading skills told me something far outside the norm was in play. After about fifteen minutes of questions, the vice principal asked me to wait while he went to get the school principal. It seemed that one of the two chemistry teachers for the school had given notice that he was leaving. A book publishing company had offered him a job at about twice what he was making. This was before teachers unions, when teachers really were not well paid. (The salary, inflation-adjusted to the present time, was about seventeen thousand dollars per year.) The school was unable to get a replacement on short notice. The school year had already started, so that applicant pool was gone. In just a few days the students were not going to have a teacher—then I walked in with a degree in chemistry, plus summer camp teaching experience with kids and leadership skills in directing university student groups.

The principal arranged a meeting for the next morning with the superintendent of the school district that consisted of five high schools. Our 9:00 A.M. meeting on Friday morning went very well. During the interview, I explained several full- and part-time jobs I had held while working at the university. One of those jobs was working for the university's registrar ("Dr. Hill") five days per week during the regular school year and then leading student crews during the major spring and fall student registration process. The superintendent told me that Dr. Hill was a friend and he would have to call him. It was interesting that while telling me this, he was studying my face for any response in my expression. I often wondered whether he really did know Dr. Hill that well or whether that was part of an interview technique. It was almost as if he expected me to waffle in some respect.

I was back at my parents' home when the superintendent called at about 2:30 in the afternoon. He told me that my degree, transcript, and references all checked out and that the school district would like to hire me. He asked that I come back to the administrative center by 4:00 p.m. to sign various papers and to pick up the curriculum guide. I did so, and in the process, he told me that he would like me to start on Monday morning. He explained that I would have the weekend to prepare. Monday morning, the school principal would come in an hour earlier than normal to show me the classroom and to make introductions. That was one fast "you are hired and start now" adventure.

The teaching was great training for future business. A business, or perhaps I should say any successful business, is all about people. How do you get customers, employees, and suppliers to do what you want while moving the whole toward a goal? When teaching, your goal could easily be to have the students learn the subject matter. You have a mix of students. Some students are serious about learning, some want to be the class clown, some are just hoping to squeak by with the least possible effort, and a few couldn't care less about anything. Your challenge as a teacher is to get the maximum results from the maximum number of students. That should sound a lot like running a business.

I would later apply this solution to business. You set a very high standard and move the group to accomplish the challenge with personal fire, enthusiasm, generous praise, and recognition of those who meet and exceed your challenge. *You stimulate enthusiasm, and that enthusiasm becomes contagious.* You appeal to people's sense of self-value and help them have something to be proud of. This worked in high school, and it later worked really well in business. In business, the addition of a paycheck was a nice added incentive. However, to be fair, I must point out that the paycheck was only the hook. People almost always want to do well, and people who want to achieve more always drive the whole company toward excellence. Let me tell you some of the things that we did to stimulate that type of contagious enthusiasm in the classroom.

The textbooks were thirty years old. That may not have been a problem for a subject such as English, but in a rapidly evolving subject such as chemistry, it was inexcusable. I scrapped the book and taught college lecture–style for the first three weeks while the business typing class practiced by preparing a new textbook. After getting a copy of what the state wanted in the curriculum, I took several sample textbooks, plus my college books, and arranged the subject matter in an order that covered the state curriculum. I rewrote many sections and also copied a few sections from the many books. I rationalized that with so many sources I would not be violating copyright laws. At least that is what I told myself. The pages were then copied on standard 8 1/2 × 11–inch paper, and in three weeks each student had his or her own personal book. They could even write in this book, unlike the normal high school book. It was different, and different sells.

We quit wasting time on the busywork assignments and homework that really had little purpose. Homework was assigned with the answers already provided but was not collected or graded. The reason for the students to do the homework was that 20 percent of the next exam would be verbatim from the homework. Some students started helping other students who could not get the answers overnight. More of a shared camaraderie began to develop. Before the exam, most students who were concerned about grades carefully reviewed all the past homework. They learned the material far better than from a typical homework assignment. This lesson was later applied to business. *It is hard to force people to do what you wish to be done, but with incentives, most people will do much more on their own.*

I deliberately created some situations in the classroom that would get the other high school students to ask the chemistry students what was happening in the class. A little ammonium hydroxide was splashed on the heater just outside the class door, thus creating a strong odor that permeated the whole hall. A dense dark brown nitrogen dioxide gas was created in the closed classroom until it reached a depth of about eighteen inches. When the doors to the hall were opened two minutes before the class-change bell, the dense gas rolled out the doors and down the halls and caused some concern as the floor became obscured under the dense gas. The other students in the school just had to know what was going on. That provided attention for my students as they had a chance to explain.

I learned that creating situations where people get attention from others greatly enhances their self-satisfaction and their performance. *The lesson was not so much about how to get reluctant people to perform as it was about getting people to want to perform.*

A changed classroom procedure new to the school involved having two good students in each class take notes using copy paper. The notes were filed by the period of the day and the date. If students missed a day and wanted makeup information, they could simply look in the file cabinet for the missing day or days. I did not waste my time, and the process seemed to drive a "no BS, get it done now" attitude. *The lesson learned here that became important in my later business was to delegate. Give people some of the tasks you are doing and let them do them.*

After about seven weeks, two students in an adjacent study hall asked whether they could sit in the back of the class in a few of the empty seats. I always thought that study halls were an unmitigated waste of time. These students wanted to learn something without looking for a grade, and that was exactly what I thought they should do. This would be much like a college course for audit purposes only. I got approval from the school principal, and our class had two new students.

I suppose I should have anticipated what was to follow. Before the week was out, the two became four. A week later, the four became seven, and a week later, it was standing room only.

As the room became more crowded, I learned another future business lesson. *Excitement builds and a sense of importance is imparted when the space becomes limited.* As the classroom filled to standing room only,  the excitement level reached a new height and became contagious. As more students got caught up in the excitement, that excitement rose to ever-higher levels. Think of the feeling at a sporting event with only 25 percent of the space filled compared with the electrifying feeling at the event that is so crowded you can hardly get in.

Later in my business, when I led meetings, I made sure that the number of seats was limited, with standby chairs close by and ready to be added. If attendance was light, the meeting still looked full, and if we had the number we thought would be there, the act of bringing in more chairs helped create the feeling that what we were doing was very important. I owe that lesson to the study hall kids! It is strange to realize that there can be so many similarities between what it takes to be an inspirational teacher and what it takes to start and grow a business. It is not so much about control—although that is absolutely necessary—as it is about leadership. *A huge element in leadership is creating the atmosphere where people are proud of what they are doing and are caught up in the enthusiasm to do even better.*

Lessons from the Navy

When in command, command!

When I took the teaching job, the school superintendent had called the Navy and they had agreed to delay my reporting date until just after the school year. However, shortly afterward, the Navy ordered me to report in February as originally scheduled. Well, most folks know that trying to change the government is a daunting task. So there I was, off to Officer Candidate School in Newport, Rhode Island. I had no idea what my lifetime career would be. However, I was about to learn more lessons and more skills that would be most important in business.

One new and surprising lesson was an understanding of the law. I was finishing the officer training school and about to receive my commission when the list of assignments came out. I was to report to an aircraft carrier deployed in the Mediterranean Sea, immediately after an additional four-month training at the Navy's law school. That seemed like one hell of an improvement over a rice paddy in Southeast Asia, though I never did understand why—with my chemistry background—the Navy assigned me to law school. When I reported on board, the ship's captain knew that I had completed the law school training and immediately assigned me to a special courts-martial board as trial counsel (similar to a prosecuting attorney in civilian court). We had two special courts-martial boards since an aircraft carrier often held the court cases for other ships in the task force.

The legal training was a real plus once I started a business. Although I would ultimately handle about 120 cases for the Navy, this was still only a collateral duty. Nowadays I hear people speak of multitasking as if it were something new. I assure you that the Navy made sure that any good officer had many, many duties and that all had to be performed in a timely manner and often simultaneously. It is still that way today, as my daughter Marjorie can testify. She is a nuclear engineering officer for the Navy. If we focus on this multitasking lesson, we can all realize that this is a necessary skill for almost any businessperson. Arranging, prioritizing, and deciding how to get the most done in the shortest amount of time are necessary skills. You simply have to delegate many of the tasks to others. This skill became a very valuable lesson that would later be applied to my business.

After I reported for duty, I was assigned to the engineering department for my primary duty. The chief engineer, a full commander, had just been given the assignment of implementing a computerized maintenance system for the ship that encompassed all planned or preventive maintenance as well as any corrective maintenance (failures or breakages). He needed to assign this new duty to one of the officers in his engineering department. The experienced sailors were often referred to as "old salts." The old salts in the department didn't like any part of this new unreasonable idea. They looked at the new room-sized, state-of-the-art computer with a big magnetic disk- and paper-punch card feeder and were a little terrified. The whole thing looked like a disaster waiting to happen. The old salts came up with more reasons for avoiding this task than my kids had for not getting their chores done. The immediate and easy solution for the chief engineer was to give the task to the new ensign who was just reporting for duty. I am sure he also thought that it would be a waste to assign a more experienced officer because these new computer things would never be that useful.

If only the other officers in the engineering department had known just how important the ability to computerize all your maintenance operations would become, I suspect that some of the more senior officers would have jumped at the opportunity. The government paid a private consulting company an enormous amount of money to develop and test the system prior to implementation. When I left the Navy, I "borrowed" all those concepts and scheduling procedures to be used in my company's long-range planning for scheduled maintenance. Early in our company's growth, we were able to use such a scheduling system to show a level of expertise that was far ahead of that of our competitors. *Using new ideas and being technologically ahead of your competition, even a few steps, can be a tremendous advantage.*

Learning this new system required more training. So it was off to school again, this time in Norfolk, Virginia. The single most important gain from going to this new school in Norfolk was that I met my future wife. She was a Midwest college math major, newly commissioned as a marine second lieutenant communications officer. We had less than a week, but she made a very favorable impression on me.

However, duty sent us in opposite directions. I left Norfolk and flew to Istanbul, Turkey, to meet my ship that had been deployed in the eastern Mediterranean area. After a few months at sea and "showing the flag" at various ports, it was back to our home port in Mayport, Florida. Then I was off to San Diego, California, for four months of engineering school. Lyn and I met again on my way to and from the engineering school in California. Then I was back to Mayport while she went to a communication station in Okinawa, Japan. Then I went back to the Sixth Fleet in the Mediterranean, followed by the Caribbean area, the Mediterranean again, and finally Philadelphia, Pennsylvania, for out-processing when I was leaving the Navy. That nice lady, the Marine Corps second lieutenant, and I crossed paths a few times in our travels, and both of us ended up in Philadelphia and got to know each other better. I went to work for a Philadelphia company, Lyn and I got married, and I moved to Chicago with the same company and then to Indianapolis, Indiana, as the operations director for another company. We then had a new baby to pack up and transport with our moves.

My new wife and I, with a new baby, decided to take a chance and start our own cleaning service business. I gave notice to my employer. We packed our possessions in a U-Haul and moved to Greensburg, Pennsylvania, just east of Pittsburgh. We chose the area for a number of reasons, most of which were accurate but some of which proved unwarranted. Either way, it really did not matter. We had rolled the dice, and now it was a make-or-break situation. We did not know anyone in the area and had to get everything started by ourselves, with no help and not very much money to spare.

But let's get back to the lessons learned in the Navy that transferred to business. Perhaps the biggest lesson was: *When in command, command! People will not follow an indecisive leader.* Employees in any business expect the leader to be able to make decisions. Sometimes there are many right decisions, and sometimes there are no right decisions. You still have to keep the team in motion or set a new direction. Right or wrong, an unmade decision (when one is required) in the military is a lack of command ability, and in business it is the kiss of death.

In the civilian world, I am a big believer in developing a team mentality and an empowered management process.

Be careful to understand that such concepts do not mean abrogation of command. You still need to command. As a chief executive officer (CEO), you assign teams to tackle issues and report ideas back to you within a very finite time frame. You assign responsibility to individuals and hold them accountable. When it is time for a decision to be made, you do not take a vote. Far too often I have seen managers, presidents, etc., want to take a poll before giving a decision. When a decision-by-poll mentality sets in, your employees lose confidence. Your company becomes slow in responding to the changing business adventures and to business opportunities. In business, it is important to understand that each change, even if it seems to be a bad thing, is also an opportunity. Decisions are required. *A leader tries to see opportunity in each misfortune.*

The military has to weed out indecision in leadership (lack of command ability) because its work environment can produce immediate life-and-death situations. In the business world, an indecisive leader is not really a leader. He or she is simply a caretaker who prays that nothing will rock the boat. A business cannot prosper in such an environment. When decisions are made, there will be mistakes, but such errors of commission are far less destructive than the errors of omission.

Another important Navy lesson that was hard to learn for this type A personality was to let the chiefs and petty officers run their areas of responsibility. In business, that lesson translates to letting the managers and supervisors run their areas of responsibility. The leader needs to support them, help them look good, and give them the credit (all the credit), and in turn, they will help their leader look good. If people simply cannot do what needs to be done, a leader should help find something they can do with pride or, if that fails, give them the opportunity to work for a competitor.

The military advances the highest-performing individuals to the next level and then to the next level, with fewer and fewer openings to fill as one moves up the command structure. What do you think happens to the ones who get passed over for promotions? In the officer ranks, being passed over for promotion twice resulted in being dismissed from the Navy. This makes room for new people coming up the chain of command and simultaneously gets rid of some of the underperforming individuals. In some circles, we call this deadwood. But what do we do in the business world with our underperforming management staff? Far too often, we do nothing. It hurts to release people. We know these people. No one wants to fire someone, and then there is the time necessary to retrain, so the poor leader does nothing.

When the boss or leader fails to remove the underperforming individuals, the business gradually moves from a dynamic organization pushing the envelope of excellence to a company accepting mediocrity as normal operations. Such a failure is almost the same scenario as the indecisive leader who seeks only to hold on to what he or she has and hopes nothing goes wrong on his or her watch. Probably the hardest thing to do in business is to dismiss the individual who is sort of okay but who is still underperforming the job after you have done all you can to help him or her. In business, we all need to learn this lesson, and the military sets the example. With all that said, I know that I certainly could have learned this lesson better.

The McDonald's Lesson

I get to use my customer's money interest-free.

There were a few lessons I learned well before my college years that also were to have an effect on the business that I would start one day. By the time I was twelve years old, I discovered shoveling snow as a way to earn money. If I shoveled a large property with sidewalks all around, it was difficult to get the owner to cough up five dollars (inflation adjustment to the present time would be about fifteen dollars). If I shoveled a very small sidewalk, I could easily get one dollar from almost every door I knocked on. There was an extensive apartment and town house complex not far from my house, all buildings with very short sidewalks. Because they were also very close together, I could solicit, shovel, and collect for about seventeen of these extremely short sidewalks for every one big house. I would earn over three times the money with this approach. This became what I call the McDonald's lesson in business. If you sell lots of hamburgers all day, you will probably make a lot more money than if you sell only a few steaks.

McDonald's did not yet exist in my small town, but when it did, it was easy to see some of the reasons for its success. I observed what McDonald's was doing and combined that with my snow shoveling lessons to target the type of business I would start. In the cleaning business, this concept became "a small profit twenty-four hours a day, seven days a week, fifty-two weeks a year equals one whale of a lot of money."

McDonald's also used what I call a cookie-cutter growth strategy. The individual wishing to own a franchise provided the money to set up one location. McDonald's then duplicated that at another location, and then at another location, and then another. If you can use other people's money interest-free, you can grow very quickly without borrowing and investing huge sums of money.

I didn't have much money to invest and knew that if I wanted to own a business, I almost certainly would need to use others' money. The janitorial service business allowed such an opportunity. We set up a process to bill our customers on the first of the month for the services we were going to be doing that month. Because payroll expenses were paid after the work was completed, the business picked up at least a half-month cash flow with each new customer. If it were a retail business, it would be as if the supplier advanced to you the full sale price for the merchandise, including overhead and profit, and you didn't have to pay for it until it was sold.

The lesson that McDonald's provided was to make lots of sales all the time and to use others' money to expand your business.

Who Gets the Worm?

Some customers provide a far better return than others.

When I was fourteen years old, a group of eight older Boy Scouts, ages seventeen to twenty-five, planned a one-month camping trip into the Rocky Mountains. These young men were experienced backpackers and knew about camping in the wild. One week of that trip was to be at a scout camp called Philmont, in New Mexico, and then we would head north. I thought that it was a great idea and tried to convince my parents to let me go with them. My parents thought that I was far too young, but they didn't want to say a flat "no," so they came up with an idea. They said I could go but I had to earn the money. It was March, and the group would leave in June. They had one hundred percent confidence that such a sum of money was far beyond the reach of a fourteen-year-old junior high school student, especially given the very short time frame in which I had to get the money.

I found a weekend job working as a golf caddie at the Sparrows Point Country Club, which was on the shore of the Chesapeake Bay, well east of Baltimore, Maryland, and only four miles from my home. This was a time before motorized golf carts, and there was a demand for caddies. The caddies were divided into three pay groups, based on skill level. It normally took two seasons to move from entry level to the top grade.

The first thing I learned was that golfers must be at least half-crazy people. They play in the cold, they play with patches of snow on the ground, and they play at first light well before sunup. In early March, I was at the golf course by 5:15 in the morning both Saturday and Sunday. The sky was just releasing the blackness of night. The gold streaks of morning had not yet appeared. The only people to be seen were just a few of the crazies and me. The pro didn't even show up until just before 7:00 a.m., when the shop officially opened. Every Saturday morning there were two golfers who showed up prior to 5:45, and another two who came most Sundays at almost exactly 6:00. I later discovered that together, those four owned about forty-six percent of the stock of the country club.

They were so delighted that a caddie was there so early in the morning that they quickly taught me what I needed to know. They liked my enthusiastic energy and twisted the arm of the pro to quickly get me in the top pay grade. I liked the generous tips that they provided and made sure to be there early for those guys.

I was quickly learning that some customers provide a far better return than others. Because no other caddie was there, I would take both bags. We would blow through the course in about two and a half hours, walking the eighteen holes. These guys played serious golf. They never took practice swings and always had the ball in the fairway. By a little after 8:00 a.m., we had finished the course, and very few of the caddie staff had arrived. After a very brief delay for the few caddies who were available to take their turn, I could pick up another group.

This next group was almost always a foursome. The foursomes were naturally slower, and other people on the course slowed things down even more. This second trip would take about five hours, but I was still getting paid for two bags and still had time for another round later in the day. This schedule set up some fourteen-hour days, but I had a goal, and it was fun. If I had stayed home, I would have had to clean house or be assigned some equally noxious job.

It wasn't long before I was coming home with two hundred and fifty dollars for a weekend (adjusted for present-day dollars). It took my parents about four weekends to realize that I was going to make the target with a very comfortable margin. They still thought that I was way too young, but because they had promised, the die was cast. I went for a month in the Rocky Mountains and hiked through three states. I was by far the youngest and least experienced of the group. However, I had been carrying two golf bags and walking through not less than thirty-six holes of golf each Saturday and Sunday. That kind of exercise left me in great shape to carry more than my share of the load.

I did not know it at the time, but the experience taught me a valuable lesson to be applied later in starting and growing a business. I am tempted to use the old cliché that the early bird gets the worm, but that thought is incomplete. The lesson was more like: *Some people came in late and waited for something good to happen. Other people, who came early, attacked the job with vigor, put in extra effort, and were rewarded far more than those who just showed up and went through the motions.* In business, that extra effort separates you from your competitors. Since all business is competitive, the difference between a successful business and one that just survives is often the extra effort.

I hope it is obvious that it is effort that leads to results and that it has very little to do with luck. After we had a successful business, I would sometimes encounter envious people who made comments such as, "You sure were lucky to be in the right place at the right time." One envious detractor even went so far as to emphatically assert, "You have to admit a successful business is really a matter of luck." I always try to be nice to people, so I replied that I understood the point but I also noticed that the harder people worked, the luckier they became. What I would really like to have said was "You have a point. Ask any failure and they'll agree with you."

Camp Director

A staff will quickly lose confidence in a boss who will not step up and take charge.

I had joined a Boy Scout troop at age eleven and quickly became a patrol leader. Our patrol was so much more active than the others that all the new kids wanted to be in our patrol, and soon I was the senior patrol leader. With my scout experience, it was natural for me to seek a job at the scout council's summer camp. The summer after ninth grade, I got a job on the activity staff in Area II of the camp. The caddie job had already taught me something about pleasing customers. This camp had two levels of customers: the boys attending the camp and their scout leaders. I did well with both but still almost did not go back the following summer. I was sure I could get a much-better-paying job doing something else, but my dad encouraged me to go back. He insisted that he made enough money for the family and living outdoors in a summer camp was good for me.

Some people told me that what happened the next summer at my Boy Scout summer camp job was a lucky break. Maybe, but luck favors those who step up and do something. The camp's experienced activities director graduated from college with his master's degree in civil engineering and moved to another part of the country. Those were big shoes to fill. The council filled the job with a man who had taught shop at a junior high school for about twenty years. On paper he looked great. On the job he was unsure of himself. Another second-year staff member named Marvin and

I kept stepping up to help. Before long, it seemed that the new director couldn't make a decision without asking one of us what he should do. The staff quickly lost confidence. I did not yet know it, but here was a major lesson for future business: *A staff will quickly lose confidence in a boss who cannot or will not step up and take charge.* By halfway through the summer, Marvin and I ran the activities staff. The following year I was offered the job as the activities director for Area II. Marvin took on some major responsibilities in another area.

Was that luck? Maybe, but if it was, luck sure seems to favor those who step up and get something done. People who believe succeeding or not succeeding is mostly a matter of luck are the same ones who only talk about trying to do something but never seem to do it.

That year, at least one-half of the activity staff was older than me. If I hadn't done the job for most of the previous year, at my age I would never have gotten that job. That year, two of the counselors on the activity staff were schoolteachers. It must have been strange to have someone the age of their students as their boss. I know it was strange for me, but somehow we made it work. This was great training for a future business. The lesson I was learning was how to get people of different ages, different abilities, and, most of all, different egos to work together. I was successful most of the time. More of the staff began to return for multiple seasons. The experience level increased, and the staff became much more professional. The Boy Scout council really liked the team I kept together and the spirit of that team. They kept offering me more money each summer through my college years to come back as the activities director.

The experience as activities director helped to develop some leadership demeanor, which directly led to being in charge of the student work crews during my jobs at college. That allowed me to earn enough to pay one hundred percent of my own college expenses the last couple of years. The Navy liked the fact that I was the leader or supervisor for the student work crews and the fact that I was in the student government. They took me for their officer program when the competition was very intense. Was that luck? Some would say it was, but I doubt most of you would buy into that story. The circumstances might change, but the results would be similar whenever a person just steps up and gets something done.

Part II

The Illustrative and Anecdotal Stories about What Janitors See and Hear

In Part 1 of this book, I enjoyed telling you about some formative experiences that helped to provide the leadership and understanding that can be so necessary to create a successful business employing many hundreds of people. In Part 2 you will notice that the janitors are applying many of those business and life experience lessons. The narratives in Chapters 2–6 consist of many separate tales from the janitors. These are their stories.

I have enjoyed recording each of the tales and now hope you will find great enjoyment as you read the following stories about the events and adventures of the janitors. The stories are all absolutely true. Each and every tale told really happened.

The stories should evoke many different emotions. You will find pleasure, sorrow, amazement, bewilderment, delight, anger, and many more emotions, as each story is a separate story with its own place in the tides of life. The stories tell all of us about the events experienced by the very hardworking people who clean our buildings.

Chapter 2:

Sex in the Cleaning Business

Short Skirts and Long Legs

***You darn fool: you should be
giving my company a bonus.***

One of my earlier customers was a large office building for a public utility company. We had twenty people working a permanent part-time shift of four hours each evening. The building air conditioners shut off precisely at 5:00 p.m. The cleaning staff worked from 5:00 to 9:00 p.m. The summers could be hot, and that building quickly heated. Because the cleaning staff did more physical labor than any of the very few remaining administrative office employees, I did not object to our staff wearing shorts.

One very good employee asked whether she could have two months off to visit family on the other side of the country. She explained that she had a college-aged niece named Linda who needed a summer job and if the niece could have the job until she got back, that would help the niece and keep her job open, and I would have a dedicated, conscientious replacement. It seemed like a very good idea. I interviewed the niece during a weekend break, and she told me how much she wanted to help her aunt who had always done so much for her.

I normally avoided college students for summer jobs since they would quit in a moment's notice for another job paying ten cents an hour more or bail after the first three weeks with serious job performance deterioration. But this was different; it was clear she would do a good job just to help her aunt.

The young lady was about five feet eleven inches tall, with long, silky blonde hair, a brilliant warm smile with dimples, and sparkling blue eyes that were the same shade as our powder-blue smocks. She could have modeled for Victoria's Secret.

When the really hot summer days started, with the AC off, the cleaning staff shifted to shorts. Linda's smock came about a third of the way down her thigh and just barely over the short shorts under the smock—just close your eyes and picture a gorgeous, well-built super-model with nothing but legs showing below a short smock.

The department head for this utility company called me to his office one midsummer day. This man had the personality of a long-dead log, and he had his two principal assistants with him.

He started out telling me, "We have a very serious problem." I had no idea what he was talking about, and still he rambled on and on, then telling me how his company's entire engineering department was staying late every night.

It was then that I noticed an assistant named Marty standing behind his boss and trying to keep a straight face. I wondered about that. Still, I did not understand what the department head was talking about, but I assumed that somehow our cleaning procedures or timing of service was interfering with their operation.

I started to apologize to the department head for any overtime we were costing him. He rather indignantly cut me off and in a surly manner said, "These engineers are all on salary." I took a deep breath and thought to myself, "Okay, he has a burr in his pants about something." But I just smiled and replied, "Our customers are very important to us, and I will do whatever we have to do to correct the problem. But help me understand what we are doing that is impeding your engineers."

He shot me an "Are you stupid?" sort of look and said, "It's that girl. All the engineers are staying to watch that girl." Then I knew! Even though I had not yet seen the pale blue smock barely covering her short shorts, I knew!

When the department head said "it's that girl," I saw Marty trying hard not to laugh. He was standing behind his boss. I sometimes wonder how people get their jobs. This director seemed so foolish in so many ways. Marty was the sane one in that group of three. Marty saw me start to smile, and surely he knew what I wanted to say. I was thinking, "The engineers are all on salary, and they are all working late without extra pay. You darn fool. You should be giving my company a bonus or at least a real big 'thank you.'" Then I saw Marty gently shaking his head from side to side while gritting his teeth. I could almost hear his silent voice saying, "Charlie, don't say it; please, don't say it." I bit my lip and kept a straight face and said, "I understand and will take corrective action."

Linda started wearing jeans, but a good percent of the young engineers still found it desirable to work late.

That Service Is Not in Your Specifications

Oh, my God! What are we going to do?

The third customer we had was a manufacturing plant of a Fortune 500 company. My company was very new, and I was wearing all the hats. About eight months into the service, our crew chief called and explained that a situation had developed. He explained he had been looking for Sally. Sally was the new employee who started weeks earlier, and he wanted to let her know the customer had a special request for one of her rooms. Each person had a very detailed schedule (i.e., 6:00 p.m. check-in; 6:05 clean ABC office; 6:11 clean XYZ office; etc.). You get the idea. Paul knew where Sally was supposed to be, but she wasn't there.

There was a light coming from around the corner and down the hall near the entrance to some production areas. Paul explained that he walked down the hall while calling Sally's name and saw the night foreman come out of the end office and immediately turn away to a door out into the production areas. Since the light was still on, Paul continued down the short remaining hallway and, upon opening the door, found Sally hurriedly trying to get the rest of her clothes back on!

Now, Paul was very much a proper religious gentleman, and I know he must have been profoundly shocked. So I did not know exactly what to say, and I asked Paul what he did. Paul looked me in the eye and replied, "I said, 'Excuse me!'"

By the time Paul was telling me the tale, the shift was over, and Sally had already left. She couldn't get out fast enough. It turned out that Sally and the night foreman were old high school sweethearts, both now in their forties.

This was something that would require some consideration. Do we accuse the Fortune 500 company's trusted night foreman? Does Sally then respond with sexual harassment charges? I decided that this needed to go to our customer's attention at once. Early the next morning, I sat in the office of Ivan Barnes, the human relations director. Ivan was a person I felt comfortable with from my close association with his company. Nevertheless, I was a bit red-faced telling him what had happened.

Ivan looked astonished. He rolled his chair back toward the wall behind his desk, took a deep breath, and said, "Oh, my god! Chuck, what are we going to do?" Well, sometimes the devil just gets hold of me, and I couldn't resist teasing. So, I looked Ivan dead in the eyes and with my most serious face said, "Well, Ivan, the very first thing we have to do is raise our prices. This level of service was not in your specifications."

There was a long moment of stunned silence, until I began to crack a smile. Then, Ivan opened a big grin and said, "Okay, okay, now let's get serious."

Sally called off work the next evening, and the next, and the next. We replaced her, and our company had sidestepped a big potential problem. Unfortunately for Ivan, his night foreman had no intention of disappearing. Ivan had become sensitized to the improprieties of this individual and he began to suspect other problems as well. It took him three months to have a solid case. It seemed the foreman was also hitting on some of the company's female employees. Ivan thanked me for alerting him. That foreman could have caused some very serious problems.

Has Anyone Seen This Butt?

We are off the hot seat.

One of my customers had a mystery. It seemed someone on the day shift found several Xerox copies of someone's bare butt in a trash can by the Xerox machine. Perhaps the party was making multiple copies in order to get it right. Naturally, the customer assumed it had to be the cleaning people. The cleaning people were always the first suspects.

There were two executives walking around the building and staying late to compare butts against the Xerox copies. If you wish to imagine something really funny, just try to picture two stiff and proper executives trying to compare butts without being obvious. How you actually get a definitive picture when people are still wearing their clothes beats me. For that matter, comparing the subtleties of bare butts is way beyond where I want to go.

These two executives were on a crusade. They even set up a secret night surveillance camera, and sure enough, someone was stupid enough to repeat the exposure. I wasn't surprised when the culprit was not a cleaning person.

Now, who do you think was Xeroxing their butt? Everyone in that building was really surprised. The secret "butt copier" was a young and pretty security guard, and I have to admit that she did have a really cute butt.

You could say that it really was picture perfect. You could also say that after the perpetrator was apprehended, our company was off the hot seat.

I know that almost all of you just assumed that it was some guy. Thirty years in the janitorial business has taught me that sometimes the gals can be rather spirited. Ladies' restrooms almost always had far more and more explicit graffiti than the guys' restrooms.

Wet Mop across the Face

Good for Edith.

Edith was a short and feisty fifty-year-old lady who spoke with an Italian accent. She worked for us at a newspaper printing company. Some of her work involved a restroom in a far section of the building. When she was cleaning the men's restroom, a "closed" sign was placed on the door, and the cleaning cart was left just inside the door, to block the entrance. An alternate restroom was just around the corner. One male employee kept ignoring the closed sign, moving the cart, and finally coming into the restroom when Edith was cleaning. He would drop his pants to use a urinal.

Edith warned him more than a few times to act responsibly. One day he came into the restroom and dropped his pants to his knees. Edith had had enough, and she swung her wet mop right across his face. Germicide-laced water with printer's ink ran down his face and across his shirt.

He was such a mess he had to tell some inquisitive coworkers that Edith hit him with a mop. Later that day, part of the story got to our customer's general manager. He read me the riot act. The phone almost blistered, as he demanded to know how any of our employees dared hit one of his people with a wet mop.

After I discovered what provoked the mop across the face, I told the general manager the complete story. The next morning he sat Edith down in his office. He wanted to hear the whole story firsthand. Edith was still upset, and she could be passionate. The fire in her eyes must have been a sight to behold. Next, it was the employee's turn to explain to the general manager what had happened.

Later, a secretary told me that the closed doors rattled and shook as the general manager roared! It seemed that his mother was a feisty little Italian lady just like Edith, and it really hit home. A few days later, the customer's employee quit, as the story circulated around the facility and his level of personal embarrassment rose. This was before the sexual harassment laws were so prevalent, but Edith didn't need those laws. She had her own solution. Good for Edith. It was not our company's recommended procedure, but I still say, "Good for Edith."

Four-Wife Rotation System

A most peculiar approach to marriage.

I had been a Navy officer, traveled to lots of places, and seen many different people and their cultures, but some employees in our company surprised me with their wife rotation system. Every six months or so, they would switch.

The arrangement came to light when a company secretary named Shirley was checking payroll deductions and called to make sure some information was correct for our health program. She was told Bill wasn't there. Shirley then asked that he call her when he got back home and was told, rather matter-of-factly, "Oh, he is staying with Cathy now."

That's when we found out that there were four couples (three were employees of our company), and they just switched partners about every six months. That meant they should be back with the original husband or wife every two years—except they did not always go in the same order.

Yes, there were kids, but it all seemed to work out. They seemed like one family, all related to each other, and I guess they really were. Sometimes the wives moved to another apartment, and sometimes the husbands moved. The four couples kept to themselves (as far as I know), and they all seemed to get along. It was the most peculiar approach to marriage that I had ever seen.

Sunday at the Office

The janitors often are the first to know.

Most office cleaning was done at night Monday through Friday. Some buildings were cleaned Sunday through Thursday night. Sometimes the cleaning company was in the building on a Sunday afternoon, doing some of the more time-consuming periodic cleaning that might be done only once a month or only once a quarter. Too many times an executive, senior enough to have a key, was entertaining a secretary or a young female employee in one of the offices. Perhaps they were only following the example of our ex-president Bill Clinton.

Just so you don't think that it was always one sided, there were more than a few cases of a senior female executive with a key who was entertaining a young male employee. These executives of both sexes seemed to forget that the janitorial staff had the master keys and security codes to the buildings and could be working on Sunday. Perhaps their minds were on something else?

Such an encounter was always embarrassing for the cleaning staff. The really surprising part is that so many individuals just assumed no one was going to be in the building on a Sunday, or as I later began to suspect, perhaps they really did know. Maybe the risk factor was part of the excitement, like having sex on an elevator or the outside balcony of an apartment building. I don't understand that risk factor, but I could tell you of some really wild and risky behavior going on Sundays in closed office buildings. It was also interesting to note that the behavior was seldom by the provocative flirts but often the most reserved individuals.

It is almost too bad that I can't name the names and identify the buildings without being in court for a few years. Just use your imagination and look around your own workplace. Some otherwise very proper people have secret rendezvous, and the janitors are often the first to know.

The Morning After

Bankrupt in less than two years.

Retailers are deadly serious about grand openings. They exhaust themselves in the drive for a perfect opening. A new customer with a combination night club and supper club type of retail business did not follow the general pattern. The owners were so pleased with the way things were coming together that they held a congratulations party a few days before the opening.

This was only our forth customer, and I needed to make sure it went well. My company was also so new I did not yet have any supervisors. Our cleaning people came in at 5:30 in the morning, and I was with them.

We opened the door and walked in. The place was quite a sight.

Five or six people were passed out on the tables. There were spilled bottles and glasses everywhere and two young ladies dressed only in panties. One was passed out on a table. The other was wandering around holding her head. I remember that both were rather good-looking. I probably spent a little too long checking out that scene.

52 Tales from the Janitor

Another drunk was in the restroom with his arms wrapped around the porcelain throne as if it were his last friend in the world. He was unconscious with his chin resting on the rim of the bowl.

The place was a disaster! These people partied hard but had a sloppy operation. Maybe that was part of the reason they were bankrupt in less than two years. We discontinued the service after about nine months and were very pleased that we did get paid before the bankruptcy. It wasn't the type of customer that we wanted for our growing company, but it sure did provide some interesting stories. That party was the first but not the last. Each party seemed to provide a similar morning scene. The half-naked girls always provided an eye-opener for the two fellows in our early-morning cleaning schedule. They claimed it beat the hell out of coffee.

Service with a Show

Customer service had a new nuance.

One of our customers was an insurance company that had two shifts: 8:00 a.m. to 4:00 p.m. and 4:00 p.m. to midnight. The second shift had only about one-third of the employees as the first shift and had mostly all young ladies with lower seniority. Three college boys cleaned during this shift. All three had rather athletic builds and were real hustlers. They wore very light clothing because it could get hot when they worked so quickly.

Two of the three left after they graduated, and I replaced them with two older men. A few days later the female executive in charge of the second shift called and asked me to visit. She told me she had a delicate request. I feared the worst. Perhaps one of the new men had said something offensive to some of the young girls. I held my breath as she started to explain.

It seemed that the girls wanted me to get some better-looking guys like the two who had just graduated. The executive laughed when she told me but then added, "Seriously, it did help keep the girls motivated. It gave them something to talk about instead of complaining about work, and I would appreciate it if you could see what you can do."

I transferred the two older fellows to a different location and found two young good-looking guys.

Whenever I visited with this customer, the executive and I had to laugh about the change. It was our secret. She kept telling me that the girls were definitely pleased. That group of girls sure did surprise me, and now the meaning of customer service had a new nuance.

There is probably a good management lesson somewhere in this tale. Perhaps it is that if you have a dull, repetitive job, it is good to find something to keep from being bored and disappointed in the job.

Factory Fashions

They would have paid me to keep the job.

One of our earliest customers was a film-processing plant. Not so many years ago, in a time before digital cameras, all film was taken somewhere to be developed and printed. Before the process became simple enough for very small and local one-hour processing, all film was sent to large processing centers.

Some film arrived by courier, and some arrived by express mail. It came in different-sized rolls and cartridges of many types. I never did count the number of individual items received each day, but it must have been thousands. Picture twenty containers, the size of a fifty-five-gallon drum, filled with rolls of film and you will have an idea of the volume that arrived daily.

This customer was like only one other customer. The second shift had more good-looking girls than a chorus line in Las Vegas. Perhaps it is the lack of seniority that contributes to the younger employees working on a second shift. This group was one energetic and playful crowd. The production area was air-conditioned but only slightly so.

There were too many machines and too many chemicals to keep the plant production area cool. The smell of acetic acid wafted lightly through the air, mixed with odors of various nitrates. The only cool, odor-free area was a large cafeteria that was on two different levels.

The building had been built and later expanded so that a fourth of the cafeteria was three steps higher than the rest of the floor. It was like a natural stage.

The lunchtime break was always loud and boisterous. At times it was downright rowdy. These girls had spirit. I was later told that one day one of the girls was on the stage and another on the slightly lower level called out, "Hey, Sue, show us those hot shorts." Well, Sue was full of fun. She spun around a couple of times to the cheers and laughs of the cafeteria group and then strutted back and forth across the stage as if it were a fashion show runway. The crowd howled with laughter. As Sue began to sit down, another girl jumped up and said, "These shorts are pretty cool too," and that was how the lunchtime fashion show began.

The show quickly morphed into daily contests for the best legs, the weirdest outfit, the best figure, the cutest smile, and the most revealing blouse. Each day was a new contest. The girls came up with more categories than a television game show.

There were some guys working at the plant who also used the cafeteria, but only a few. Our company had three guys for our cleaning staff. That totaled six guys and about fifty girls in the cafeteria during the lunchtime fashion show.

It wasn't long before the girls pressured the guys into rating the contestants. Some of the girls had fun teasing the more bashful and impressionable guys. These guys may have been nervous, but they loved it.

After the fashion show started, I am sure our crew would have paid me just to keep the job. We had zero employee turnovers at this location.

Chapter 3:

Great People

Janitor with the PhD

Really taught that arrogant fool some valuable lessons.

Our company had a small retail store where we had two employees cleaning from 8:00 to 11:00 a.m. One of those two employees was Bill, who was finishing his PhD in biomechanics at a nearby university. He had recently acquired a beautiful old house practically across the street from the retail store. Working at the store provided a relaxing break from his normal academically challenging environment. The money also helped with some of his fix-up expenses for the house. The work location couldn't have been more convenient, and the store had lots of attractive college girls working in sales. This was a fun job for Bill.

The store had a young and very new assistant manager with a real superiority complex. He thought he was really special. He was demeaning to almost everyone. He thought that the sales clerks were dummies and that the two janitors were even less intelligent.

The young assistant manager's shift varied during the week. When he was working from noon to 8:30 p.m., he would often come in early in the morning, while Bill was still working. The assistant manager would do some of his academic work in the employee lounge and moan about how difficult the work was. He was working on his BS degree.

One morning, when Bill was finishing some work, the assistant manager was moaning about his schoolwork louder than usual. He was really just trying to inflate his own ego and make himself feel important.

Everyone in the lounge had had just about enough of this pompous assistant. One of the young ladies on the staff who just couldn't take it any longer winked at Bill and silently whispered, "Go get him, Bill." The assistant manager had his head bent down, looking at the papers on the table. The other staff in the lounge saw and heard what was whispered. They were smiling and silently mouthing "Go, go" to Bill.

Bill was very well liked. Most of the sales staff knew that Bill was incredibly bright, and most knew that he was finishing his PhD. It seemed that about the only person who did not understand was the very new assistant manager who was too stuck up to notice much of anything.

Bill moved over next to the table where the assistant manager was working and said, "If you are having so much trouble, I will be glad to show you how to do it."

The pompous and vain assistant manager said something like, "You couldn't understand this. You're a janitor. This is hard stuff." Bill reached over, picked up the assignment sheet, and answered the problems, without a calculator. He then started writing out the procedural steps as fast as his hand could write. He provided the astonished assistant a paper trail to the correct answers.

The dumbfounded assistant manager did not know what to say, and it would not have mattered if he had tried to say anything. The employees in the lounge were laughing too much to have heard anything, and the laughter got louder by the minute.

The store manager was a really great fellow. He thanked Bill for teaching his pompous assistant something about attitude and underestimating people. I always hoped that the store manager was right and that our janitor had really taught that arrogant fool some valuable lessons. Unfortunately, the assistant was transferred shortly thereafter. We never did find out whether he matured to be the kind of person we all could have liked.

The "Ace" in a Walker

His only absence was excused.

I had an opening for a floor-polishing job in a department store. The company was still new, so I was doing the hiring. One person who showed for the interview actually came into the store with a walker that had two wheels and two posts. Some of the other applicants snickered at the thought of this fellow applying for a job that required three hours of moving around the store while polishing floors.

When I actually hired Gahlem Shapel, the applicant with the walker, and rejected several healthy-looking younger men, they were not sure I was in my right mind. The store's manager told me he was shocked. He didn't know what to say, but because his store's appearance had so drastically improved since our company started, he couldn't wait to see how this was going to work.

I saw something in Gahlem the others had not seen. Gahlem was about sixty-one years old and had been widowed for about ten years, with no children in the area. He had spent forty years at the same heavy industry manufacturing plant before retiring. He knew what it was to punch a time clock and to actually work. He also wasn't going to be transitory. He would be at the job for a long time, and all companies need long-term employees.

In this store, corporate management had decreed that no propane-powered polishers were to be used. We were required to use battery-powered polishers. Those battery machines were about the size of a grocery cart, with the two nicest handles you could find. It was just like Gahlem's walker. It provided support, and he could lean on it. Actually, it was much more stable than his walker.

The single hardest thing to teach a person running one of these battery-powered 2000-rpm polishers was to slow down. The high-speed pad needed time to soften the floor finish (commonly misnamed floor wax) and to smooth that finish to the mirrorlike look so cherished by retailers.

I didn't have to tell Gahlem to slow down. For that job, his bad leg was not a handicap, and he brought so many positives that it would take pages to tell. He was always the first to arrive at the job. If someone had a car problem, he would pick up the employee and provide transportation until the car was fixed.

Our company grew, and in that ten-year time we had an area manager for that region, so I only infrequently saw Gahlem or the rest of the crew at that site. He had a phenomenal attendance record. He worked almost ten years for our company and never missed a single scheduled workday.

When Gahlem didn't show up one morning, the crew covered for him and they didn't even tell our own area manager.

The next morning, two of our employees stopped at Gahlem's house just to check on him. He had died in his sleep. We logged his first and only absence as excused. His work site was about a five-hour drive from my home, and I made a point of being there for his funeral. Gahlem was so appreciated that everyone missed that old gentleman who did such a superb job. Everyone at the store who could be there was there, including the original store manager, who became a regional director for the chain. He told me that he had learned so much from Gahlem, who had helped him grow into the job he now had.

The Ugly Duckling

Fifteen years of thank-you letters.

The first out-of-town customer we had was a retail store. If you do a great job in one location, they almost drag your company to other locations. It is a good way to expand business but leaves you wondering how you can effectively service such a customer when that customer is too small to have a true on-site supervisor. We needed three people for a three-and-a-half-hour shift six days per week (before Pennsylvania stores remained opened on Sundays).

Our company was still so new we did not have area supervisors or area managers. I still had all those hats. Although the store was only about a ninety-minute drive away, I was very concerned about what I could do quickly if someone was sick or one of the three employees quit after the first few days. In our industry, thirty percent turnover within the first two weeks of a new account was certainly possible.

After the first few weeks, things would settle down and turnover for our company would drop to well below 15 percent per year. But those first couple weeks could have left me really vulnerable. I decided to try using the state's job service (unemployment office) to screen people from help wanted ads I had run in the newspaper.

When I came to the job service office to do the interviewing, there were only seven people to interview, and three were clearly unacceptable. I hired the three I needed, and feeling really vulnerable with no backup available, I offered a temporary two-week job to the fourth person. He was a young man named Tom.

Normally, I avoided young people, as their performance often dropped rapidly after the first week or two and the turnover was much higher. But I was between a rock and a hard place. If one of the three brand-new employees didn't work out, I had no one else to call for an interview, without going through the time-consuming process of placing a newspaper ad, setting up interviews, and screening. It was also too far away to send a trusted individual who was already working for our company in the geographic area where we started the business and had more people resources.

Tom seemed a less-than-sterling choice. He had dropped out of high school. He had a birth defect that caused him to hobble badly when walking. He was overweight and had the worst case of eczema I had ever seen. Just describing how scaly and bloody his face and arms looked would make most people shudder. I thought I could give Tom something to do that was, for the most part, beyond our specifications. That way, I would get an "atta boy" from our customer while giving myself a bit of a reserve for the unexpected (maybe that was also a CYA move, "cover your ass").

For almost two weeks, Tom did everything I asked and so appreciated the job. I knew I would feel bad when the two weeks that I promised were up. Then the bomb burst. The most accomplished individual I had hired and appointed as crew chief for this new customer told me he had just accepted a job with the Pennsylvania Department of Transportation. The wages and benefits were well beyond our ability to match. Government, supported by a compulsory tax system, can provide benefits that are well in excess of small business start-up companies.

I decided to keep Tom as the third person on the three-person team, despite his physical appearance and the fact that he was a slow learner. By this time, the store had accepted him being there, and while he was a bit slow in learning new tasks, he did just exactly what I asked. I taught him to buff floors using a thirty-one-inch electric plug-in buffer. It was the largest plug-in machine ever made and state-of-the-art for its time.

Day after day, Tom learned and became better with the job and the machine. He had never had a job before, and this job was so important to him. He brought his mother and uncle to the store after his work shift to proudly show them what he had been doing. I later learned Tom's dad had abandoned his mom and him when he was at a very young pre-school age. Tom still thought he was partly to blame!

School and just growing up can be horrible experiences for those who are mentally challenged and with physical handicaps, and so it had been for Tom.

Now, Tom had his first job, and everyone could see the appearance of the store improving almost daily. Tom was so proud; he introduced his mom and uncle to the salespeople and the store management. Then something totally unexpected happened. Perhaps wiser people would know it was possible, but I am still at a loss for the words to explain the magnitude of what transpired.

Tom's lifelong eczema began to recede. His face and arms began to clear. The really ugly puffy swelling began to disappear. His doctor reduced the medication, then reduced it again, and then eliminated it, and still he kept getting better.

Within one year, only the very faintest signs remained of what had once been so disfiguring. Tom stood taller, dragged his leg less, held his head high, began to smile at other people, and even started joking with some of them. The change was beyond words. The people who knew Tom only one year before could no longer recognize him. He had to tell them his name. Even then, some still doubted.

Tom needed more than our permanent part-time job, so I helped him apply for a full-time school custodian job. You remember my comment about the scope of government wages and benefits? Tom got the job. I had to replace him, but it was worth it to see this young man go forward. For about fifteen years afterward, I would get an annual thank-you letter from his mom.

I learned the awesome power imparted to an individual when that person acquires a sense of pride, self-worth, and confidence. I suppose I always knew a person's attitude influenced his or her mental state of mind, but I never dreamed of the dramatic changes that could be produced in physical appearance.

Big Bag of Money!

Several people were just gone and nobody was talking.

When the company was still very new, an employee named Betty called me at home at about 8:00 p.m. She was very nervous and wanted to tell me about money she found at this bank customer. I said, "Okay, Betty, just leave a note for Mr. Smith" (our specific contact at the bank). She stuttered a bit and implored me to please come and look at it so she didn't get into trouble. So I agreed, mostly because I didn't want her to feel ignored. Boy was I in for a surprise!

The money she was talking about was in a big brown grocery bag, two-thirds full. I could see neatly wrapped stacks of twenties and fifties. Just try to imagine how much money would have been in that bag!

I called our customer contact (a senior VP) at his home and explained what had happened. He came to the building at about 10:00 p.m., looking not at all happy. When he actually saw the bag, his face changed from various shades of bright red to paste white and back to red. He called the security company to get a bypass number to open a small storage safe and locked up the bag until morning. A time lock prevented opening the main safe.

I was told that the next morning was not pretty. When the proverbial fecal matter hits the fan, it can get really messy.

I know I was smart enough to stay far, far away. Within two days, several people were just gone, and nobody was talking. Betty got a special thank-you and a government bond purchased in her name.

Surprising Talent

A better group of people would be hard to find.

There is always the tendency to assume that people doing cleaning jobs are doing so because they can't do other things. Permanent part-time cleaners perform much of the cleaning. Offices are often cleaned in the early evening, and retail stores are cleaned in very early morning hours before the stores open for business. Let me tell you about some of the day jobs that our cleaning people had (I hope you are as surprised as most people): PhD college professor, student for advanced degrees, accountant, zoning commissioner, schoolteacher, town mayor, union leader (retired), computer trainer, postal supervisor, manufacturing company foreman, farmer, actress, professional musician, church minister, millwright, volunteer firefighter, electrician, union business manager (retired), author, secretary, student for trades, salesperson, and police officer.

These people were also instrumental in helping their communities on so many different levels it is difficult to remember. Some things included the grandmother who kept several neighborhood children during the normal working day, without pay. She did this so the moms could help the family income.

There was the fellow who loaded up one of our company buffers each Saturday (with our donated chemicals and parts) so he could clean and polish the floor of his church. He would not allow the church to pay him. He was also a church deacon, and it was just his way of helping. Several people volunteered for Meals on Wheels, Big Brothers Big Sisters, the Boy Scouts, food banks, the YMCA, and the YWCA, and others served as foster parents, school guards, etc.

I'm sorry that I can't list all the good things I should remember, and I am embarrassed that so many more have been forgotten. A better group of people would be hard to find.

Part-Time People Deserve Benefits

Definitely not a yes-person.

When the company was started, the employees were almost exclusively permanent part time. As we grew, the supervisors and managers were full time but salaried. Benefits were still not much of an issue.

Times changed, and we increasingly had more full-time employees for whom our company was the primary or only source of income. It was also becoming more difficult to hire new people without offering a benefits package.

Our retention was excellent, but recruiting new employees was increasingly challenging as the economy roared ahead. At a company manager meeting, I brought out the idea of adding vacation pay and holiday pay for our increasingly full-time hourly workforce.

Cathy was a feisty and uninhibited site supervisor. She was extremely emphatic that the long-term permanent part-time people—and not just the full-time people—should also get vacation pay and holiday pay. I had learned to appreciate Cathy. She definitely was not a yes-person. But to her credit, she was almost always right. She showed me a big weak spot.

If we provided vacation pay for forty-hour people, what about those working thirty-eight hours or thirty hours or twenty hours? What about those who were forty hours per week but were reduced to thirty-five hours per week during the course of a year or the reverse? I was going to have to go back to the drawing board. This project was not going to be so simple.

I had an idea of how to accomplish the benefits program for both full-time and part-time employees. I carefully outlined what I wanted and asked our industry computer software provider whether it could work. The people there said they thought they might be able to do it and also thought they could probably keep the cost to fewer than thirty-five thousand dollars. After that shock, I thought a defibrillator might be in order.

Terry, our office manager, and Ann, our payroll secretary, thought that they could do it themselves and took to the task. These two and my wife, Lyn, acting as chief financial officer, had the project done and tested in three days while still doing all their other work. Great people can accomplish great things if you let them have at it.

The way our special vacation program worked was unique in our industry. For our type of company, it was far superior to any program used by any of our competitors, and it helped to provide a competitive edge for our company. It is very important that administrative procedures be simple and easy to apply.

Let me tell you how this program worked. On the anniversary date of hire, the computer would look back at the total number of hours worked and divide that total hour number by fifty-two weeks per year. The computer then multiplied the average hours worked over the past year by the current rate of pay. The resulting vacation pay was included on the next paycheck. Let's examine the benefits of this approach:

- Only long-term employees get the benefit. (You quit and you are out—no prorating.)

- Field supervisors and managers do not have to continuously monitor who has been working how long and who has to use vacation now or lose it. (Losing vacation time really upsets people.)

- People who call off of work have fewer total hours in the year and therefore have less vacation pay.

- A leave of absence also reduces total hours for the year for vacation pay.

- Employees get a check, and some would rather get a refrigerator. People still get vacation, but they get the check up front.

- People could put the money in the bank until they need it for a vacation, prepaid airline tickets, Disney Park accommodations, etc.

- Managers can give any employee time off without double-checking to find out what vacation time, if any, remains.

- The office administrative staff has almost zero burdens about vacations.

- Offering benefits is a recruiting tool advantage over competitors without benefits.

- Customers like the idea that we pay benefits, and when our salespeople show how little it adds to the cost of our service, they almost always agree to add the cost to our contracts.

Good people produced the program, and the company's workforce loved it. Special thanks to Cathy, Terry, Ann, and Lyn, who did such a great job—and perhaps to all the people who spread the word, thereby helping us recruit new employees. We also need to thank customers who quickly added the cost to our service payment.

I should also point out that not everyone stayed until his or her anniversary date. Any unpaid vacation pay would then accrue to the company, although the retention rate was so good this was not a big savings for the company. Our retention rate was a great many times better than our industry average, which also greatly reduced our hiring and training costs.

Ask and You Shall Receive

People who make a company great always volunteer.

A janitorial service company has employees who work at the customers' locations that are often separated by many miles or even several states. As a result, the team camaraderie that can be so beneficial to any organization is difficult to invoke.

A company newsletter is one approach to help bridge the gap. If a newsletter is constructed with care, it can accomplish many things. It helps people working at distant locations have a sense of being part of a single company. It helps spread the good news when the employees do good things at our different customers' buildings. It also helps people to understand that promotions are happening within the company and to understand the career possibilities that can be important to them.

People liked to see their names in the newsletters, so when they passed our professional certification (training) program, we published their names. We added their birthdays and anniversary years of service. We featured awards and complimentary letters from our customers that named employees. All such things helped to bind together all of the people in the remote customer locations into one company, instead of a series of separate work sites.

We could also share our newsletters with our customers and target prospective customers. We really wanted customers and potential customers to know what a stable workforce and great company we had.

The need for this newsletter program was increasingly apparent. The CEO cannot personally do all the many tasks that need to be done, so I asked for volunteers. Karen and Norm stepped up. They didn't just help; they totally took over the project and created a really great newsletter. Our international trade association has an award for the best newsletter of our member companies. The newsletter that they created was in the final three for the award almost every year. My total required contribution was an article titled "Message from the President" for each issue. I often wrote other articles just for the fun of it but left my name off those.

Bosses cannot do everything. They have to ask others, and the people that will make the company great will respond.

Four Old Fellows

After that, hell would have to freeze over . . .

I had the great fortune to have four retired men work for the company at a seventy-thousand-square-foot retail store. They each had spent thirty-plus years in manufacturing jobs and retired with pensions but still wanted to do something. Our 7:00–10:00 a.m. cleaning job was perfect. They got out of the house, their wives got a break, and they earned some extra money. These four were intelligent and attentive employees who always tried to do their best and seldom missed a day of work. Any employer with such people would be really blessed.

About three and a half years into this contract, the store had a new assistant manager. She had been promoted and transferred from another location. She thought that a manager had to be a demanding, aggressive bully and verbally beat up employees to get results. She attacked everyone, including our four employees.

After about a month of abuse, the four got me aside during one of my visits and told me they had had enough. They were giving me a two-week notice. Nothing I said could make them change their minds. I knew that there was no hope of replacing them with better people or even with people that were close to as good as they were.

There was a discontent rumbling through the store's sales staff as well. That poor assistant store manager had no idea how to talk to people or how good she had it, and no one could reason with her. I thought, "What can I do?" I really needed to keep these four people. What would you do?

Think about it for a minute and see whether you have the same idea that I had. Try to be creative and think of an "out of the box" solution.

After extending sympathy and telling the four how good they were, I talked up the idea of having some fun with the assistant manager. Because the four would be leaving anyway, I convinced them to "mess with her mind," as I called it. That phrase was to get their attention. Four old mill hands could appreciate a practical joke. They agreed to play the game I proposed.

It went like this. When the assistant manager came in the store at about 9:00 a.m., the four were to attack, preferably with Joe, our crew chief, leading the way. Instead of trying to avoid this very unpleasant assistant manager, they were to run right up to her, step in front of her so she had to stop, and say "Good morning, Mrs. Smith" and then say something like "I want to show you an area by the paint section. A customer must have had a major spill. It was a real mess, but you should see it now."

I cautioned them that they should expect her to say okay, but then she would immediately find something else to complain about. Then our four should reply, "You are absolutely right, but this had to be done today. We will get that first thing tomorrow." Then the next day, attack again and show her that whatever she had criticized was done. The point was not to try to avoid her but instead each and every day to get right in her face as soon as they saw her.

Bullies tend to beat up people who hang their heads and hide. I asked the four to attack with their heads up and with killer smiles. They could smile because they knew that they were "messing with her mind." It was a game they could play without any fear of losing their jobs. They were leaving anyway.

The store manager and I got along really well. I told him what was going on and got his blessing. He also had his problems with her but had not yet been able to get her to change her approach. After just eight days, Mrs. Smith came in the front door and saw that our crew chief was heading straight for her. She put up her hand, palm flat out, and said something like, "Stop, Joe. Everything is just fine. The store looks great, and I have to get to the office right away."

She avoided our four people for the rest of their shift. The next day was almost an exact repeat. The four old fellows decided that this was so much fun they would hold off quitting for a few more weeks.

As the assistant manager began to change her attitude, the store manager sat her down and explained what was happening and why it was happening. A big lightbulb must have gone off because the next day she held a meeting with all the staff. She included the salespeople, the cashiers, the stockroom people, and our four cleaners. She apologized to everyone and publicly thanked our four old fellows for so clearly showing her how to be a better manager. After that, hell would have to freeze over before those four would really quit.

She went on to become a store manager and later a district manager, and she often used the story of the four old fellows when teaching her new people how to be better managers.

No-Cost Training

*Let there be room for good people
to create new and better operations.*

The problem faced by all highly decentralized businesses with work sites too small for on-site human resources people or even site managers is how to train new employees. How do you keep the training up-to-date and also keep the records up-to-date? If you try to do group training at all the different sites, someone will be sick or there will be one new employee next month.

What do you do? Do you drive to a work site in another state seven hours away to do special makeup training for one permanent part-time employee? Most important, how can you ever hope to have the records up-to-date for everyone? You cannot just have the absent employee or each new employee report to a training room, as with a business that is in one location. Any serious attempt to keep training up-to-date for all employees was going to be very difficult and frightfully expensive.

Dan came to work for our company as an area manager, after twenty years as a Navy engineering officer. He volunteered for the task of developing a viable program. A few weeks later, he had a report for me. The opening statement was rather dynamic. He said, "It can't be done!"

He went on to explain that as long as we had a top-down management training program, we would have to devote large resources in time and money, and we would still have major holes. He pointed out that if we ever had a workers' compensation injury, some trial lawyer would ask the employee about training, which the employee would naturally not remember (at least after coaching by a lawyer). Unfortunately, we also most likely wouldn't have accurate enough records to prove otherwise.

Up-to-date and accurate record keeping in highly decentralized companies, such as the cleaning service industry, would seem an almost impossible job. Dan had figured out that to be successful, the training had to be driven from the bottom up. The employee had to want to do the training and then push to get it done. So how did we do it? How would you do it?

Newly hired individuals received the necessary OSHA, EPA, and right-to-know training on the first day before starting to work. Some locations also required asbestos, blood-borne-pathogen, and machine lockout training prior to starting. This was done as part of the hire process. These were safety issues, and these few things were covered before the new employee was allowed to do any work at our customers' buildings. Records of this limited training were made part of the new-hire documents.

The great bulk of the training was to be done after hiring. Our employee handbook was given to all new employees with a signed tear-out page explaining many things, including our professional certification program, the name we had given to our training program.

To complete the training, each new employee had to call the office and request that the professional certification program be sent to his or her home. This kept the manager and supervisor from being under the gun or an employee complaining that his or her supervisor failed to provide a training book. When the book left the office, it was numbered and included the employee's name. The book had fourteen chapters, with a test at the end of each chapter. The work was done at home on the employees' time. It was an open-book test: we wanted people to learn, and people learn by looking up answers.

After taking the test, they copied their answers on a second tear-out page that was mailed to the office, to be graded by our training officer. I know that you are thinking, "Why in the world would new employees ever do this?"

They did not have to complete the program, but they did so because that was how they got their first raise. We did not have to pay training time wages for our professional certification program because the employees completed the program at home on their own time. They did not have to complete the program, but they all did because they wanted the raise in pay.

Almost all companies increase an employee's pay after some introduction or probation period. Our process was simple: complete your professional certification program and you get a pay raise. Upon completion, the employees also got their names in the company newsletter. They received a professional certification patch for their uniform. They also received a laminated certificate (like a degree).

People started the program because of the pay raise, but the recognition was always more important, especially to some who had never had any recognition for any success.

What did the company get? Each employee completed

training without constant badgering and to a degree of understanding that our competitors could only marvel at. Our salespeople could proudly show prospective customers a level of training that no other competitor was doing.

We had copies of training tests in each employee file in the employees' own handwriting. We once had an employee who was dismissed for smoking in our customer's building. At an unemployment compensation hearing, he claimed he did not read that part of the handbook and the supervisor did not warn him he couldn't smoke in our customer's building. But the unemployment compensation hearing was over when we introduced the test page from our training manual. There, in his own handwriting, was the answer "No smoking in any customers' buildings."

Dan deserves the lion's share of credit for having the clarity of thought to know we needed a bottom-up-driven program and for writing much of the training book. Norm assisted with some of the writing and most of the test questions, and then he became our corporate training officer.

Business owners and executives need to allow good people to create new and better operations for their companies. This bottom-up training program worked perfectly and was a huge asset for our company.

Chapter 4:

Hard to Believe...
But True

Workplace Tobacco

The surprising things people will say.

Long before no-tobacco policies were standard, our company had a policy of no tobacco products being used by our employees in any of our customers' buildings. One night at a twenty-seven-story downtown metropolitan office building, the site supervisor was looking for two young men who were part of a special project team. That night, the two were stripping and waxing a floor near an employee lounge and were set to take a break in the lounge while the floor dried between the coats of floor finish.

When the site supervisor was making her rounds, she found the floor drying, but the employees were not in the lounge. There was a nearby door shut and locked from the other side, and her master key wouldn't open the door. That was unusual because that door was always open, so she got security to come up to the floor and open the door. There were two surprised employees sitting on the floor and smoking.

The supervisor had started into these two about being where they shouldn't be and about our company's no-tobacco policy. Just then, one of the young men blurted out, "But, boss, this isn't tobacco; it's weed." The second young man just shook his head as if to say, "You fool." The supervisor had security escort both directly to the door. This was from a time before we had mandatory drug screening

I suppose we should never be completely surprised by what some people say. The really surprising part was that the one employee really didn't get the idea that he had done something wrong. Shocking but true.

All the Crackers You Can Eat

The tale was more desperate with each telling.

One winter, an overnight blizzard had shut down western Pennsylvania to a degree I had never seen since I moved there. I used a big four-wheel-drive vehicle to get to our office, manned the phones, and coordinated what I was sure was going to be an eventful day. The city of Pittsburgh was impassable with about three feet of overnight snow and drifts much higher in many places.

The phones were quieter than I expected. A call at about 7:30 a.m. was the first. We had a team of two people working overnight. They were scrubbing and rewaxing the floors in a retail store in what was referred to as a "lock-in." The doors were locked at 9:30 p.m. and unlocked at 7:00 a.m. when the store manager came back in the morning. In the overnight period, emergency exit doors were available but with alarms, police, and nasty results.

That morning, our people waited about a half hour after opening time, and then when no one arrived to open the doors, they called for help. I told the folks to relax and enjoy the break and reminded them that they were still on the clock.

The blizzard had provided the easiest overtime they would probably ever get. By noon, they called back again. I told them I had already checked and that none of the stores' key carriers could get through the snow. I again told them to relax. They said they were really getting hungry, and I told them to go to the employee lounge to make some coffee and get some crackers. I asked them to just record how many crackers they ate and we would cover it with the store. Again I pointed out that the overtime clock was still running.

By 4:00 p.m. they called back again. They had been eating crackers for breakfast, lunch, and supper. They had already eaten about twenty-five packs of crackers each and didn't care to ever see another cracker. They wanted to use the emergency exit. I asked them to go to the front and look in the parking lot. I asked whether anything was moving. "No!" they replied. Then I asked, "If you do get out, what are you going to do? Isn't it better to wait in a warm store than be stuck in a cold truck?" The logic was good enough to overcome the cracker phobia.

Fortunately, by 5:30 p.m. someone from the store did arrive with a helpful police escort. Our employees were able to start a slow and careful drive home. The cracker tale was something our fellows never tired of telling some new employees, and the way they told it became more desperate with each new telling.

The Thundering Herd

In a New York minute.

This is a story that begs to be told. The same public utility director of building services involved in the "Short Skirts and Long Legs" story called me another time to come to his office to discuss another serious problem. Again, his two principal assistants were there. He lectured me about our people creating a very negative impression for his company's employees.

He must have rambled on for fifteen minutes about this serious problem that would have to be solved at once. I still had no idea what he was talking about, but he was a customer, and I was trying my best to understand and be respectful.

He finally got around to telling me his very serious problem. When he came back to the building in the evening, he could see our people leaving within a few minutes of the end of the 5:00–9:00 p.m. shift. There was a long moment of silence while I tried to understand why that was a problem.

After the awkward silence, I rather tentatively said, "So the problem is that for our people to actually get out of the building that quickly, they must have already put their equipment away and washed up and been pretty much ready to punch the time clock at 9:00 p.m."

I added something like, "So you are telling me the people should have been hard at work on their respective assignments until 9:00 p.m. Therefore, by the time they put equipment away and wash up, they should not be able to exit the building for fifteen or twenty minutes after the shift." "Yes! Yes!" he bellowed as if I were really stupid.

While I was still in a partial state of shock and wondering whether I should even try to explain federal wage and hour laws, a bell in the building rang. This four-hundred-thousand-square-foot office building had a bell for dismissal! I hope this would astonish most people. I know I was shocked; it reminded me of an elementary school.

When that bell rang, a thundering herd of employees raced down the hall right past the open door to the office where we were sitting. I watched the fleeing people for a moment, and a huge smile crossed my face. I turned to my irrational antagonist and said, "I can certainly understand why your company could be concerned about such a bad example."

In a New York minute the hall was almost empty. He didn't know what to say. He finally stammered something about . . . well . . . we will talk about that later. People sure can be fascinating. The good news is that his company retired him before the end of that year, and that was probably ten years too late. One assistant had his job eliminated as a way to get rid of him, and the one good man (Marty) took over as department head. It was about time.

Raising the Dead

Al was like a SuperBall careening off the walls.

One of our most unusual customers was a mausoleum. It was a beautiful building with a bright glass and brass entrance and highly polished white marble floors. When you came in, there was a small lobby with a corridor straight ahead, another corridor to the left, and a third one to the right. Each was about fifty feet to the end wall.

The walls on each side had small front cubes, each labeled for the remains of departed loved ones. Within each of the three sections were several large easy chairs.

In the center of each corridor there were two stone-surfaced tables about eight feet long and three feet wide. Flowers were often placed on these tables during services for those who were being added to the mausoleum. The owners ran a very nice operation and among other things insisted that the marble floor be polished to a perfect shine.

Fred and Al were one of our two-person traveling crews. One day when they arrived at the mausoleum, there was what appeared to be a body lying on one of the tables. Al had to polish the floors, and he was the most easily spooked person I ever knew. He polished the first two wings before working up the courage to go into the wing with the dead body on the table.

Al went to the edge of the wall and, with great anxiety, passed as far away from the table as possible. His shoulders were flat against the wall as he quietly slid along the wall and crept past the body. His partner, Fred, was chuckling at his apprehension. He even called out, "Al, it's okay. He can't hurt you." Al finally started the buffer but always kept one eye on the body on the table.

It was about 3:00 in the afternoon, and the mausoleum was a cool and shady place. The gardener had decided to take a break and cool off for a while, and he had fallen asleep on the table. You can only imagine the scene that followed.

What Al thought was a dead body moved just a little. Al made a low guttural sound as he sucked in air. The gardener move again, and Al let out a long soft whine (try gritting your teeth together to make a noise like fear and shock).

The only way out was past the stirring body on the table. Al yelled out for his partner as he took a few tenuous steps toward the exit and tried to get past the body. He uttered a terrified cry, "Fred!" Implied in his panicked voice was "Please save me!"

When Al yelled, the gardener bolted upright and looked in his direction. Al turned back, ran smack into the wall, and knocked himself straight down to the floor. He jumped up and ran into another wall. If there is such a thing as being blinded by fear, Al had it.

The gardener's feet hit the floor, and he turned toward Al, intending to help this young man with whatever was wrong. The panic only intensified as the gardener moved toward Al. The buffer machine was running wild and bouncing off walls almost as fast as Al, with an electrical cord trailing.

Now all buffering machines have "dead man" switches to shut off the machine if you let go of the handle, but not then. Al tripped on the cord, ran into the machine, and bounced off walls again and again as the gardener moved closer.

Al was like a SuperBall careening off the walls. His blood-curdling scream was finally too scary for the gardener, who backed up toward the central lobby. Fred ran to Al's aid to calm him down and finally convinced him that the gardener was not a dead body coming to life.

Al survived the incident with only three cuts that required stitches and no broken bones but with more bruises than you would want to count, and some of those were whoppers.

Even though the gardener wasn't really dead, Al never went back to that site again. A team of wild horses could not have even dragged him past the road that led to the mausoleum.

Tasty Legal Fees

List the difference as legal fees.

Our company was a janitorial service company. While it was a much smaller part of our business, we also sold supplies and equipment primarily to businesses that were already customers. There was a really high-class resort in a nearby community that wanted sixteen hundred dollars worth of cleaning machinery. We sold the machines to that high-class resort.

Our normal customers had a standard recurring monthly invoice. Because this resort was a one-time sale, it was a couple months before we realized the bill had not been paid. We called. The managers at the resort apologized and promised to send a check shortly. Another month passed and still no check. We called again. They apologized again and promised a check within the week. By now, you probably suspect that the check is not coming. A few more phone calls and duplicate fax invoices were of no value in getting these deadbeats to pay. I was upset that these people would deliberately not pay their bill and then lie about it. A creative idea formed as I thought about the legal hoops that we would have to jump through to get a deadbeat to pay. What would you like to do in this situation?

Well, this was my solution. I took my wife, our three oldest children, and a neighbor girl who was just about like a daughter to this resort for dinner on a Friday night. My eleven-year-old son had venison smothered in truffles. Someone had pheasant under glass, another had filet mignon, and so on. I am sure you get the picture. The desserts that were ordered were the most elegant on the menu. We were finished at almost 8:30 that night.

The place was packed when the waitress brought the check. I gave her a large cash tip and a letter to the manager, authorizing them to deduct this bill from what my company was owed. My wife was so nervous at this gutsy move that she had to go to the restroom three times during dinner and twice during dessert.

I had learned that the manager always worked in an adjacent office on the resort's very busy Friday nights. As the waitress read the brief note, I said if Larry (the manager) had any problem, he could come into the restaurant to debate the issue.

I also carried cash, just in case I miscalculated what would happen. The waitress smiled, disappeared, and came back in almost no time at all. She explained that Larry had said everything was okay, the bill would be credited, and he couldn't come into the restaurant just then.

Monday morning, the resort's payables department called and said something silly like, "What should we do about this?" I suggested that several people in our company were interested in coming the next Friday. The remaining bill was paid the next day with overnight mail and included the late payment plus interest charges I had added. It came to more than the original debit on our books. We took the original invoice minus what was paid and called the difference legal fees. The "Infernal" Revenue Service never challenged that deduction. I must say it was the quickest result I ever had in the adjudication arena, and it is really nice when legal fees can leave such a good taste in your mouth.

Speed Bumps in the Road of Progress

Everyone could use the same full-length mirror.

"Speed bumps in the road of progress" was what a really talented civil engineer said about the various regulatory groups whose approval we needed to expand our office and warehouse facility. The company was a service company with work taking place at twenty million square feet of our customers' locations. Our own office and warehouse areas did not have to be too big, but we did need more space. We were growing from four thousand square feet to eleven thousand square feet.

It seemed all the different regulatory approval individuals wanted the other regulatory people to sign off first. Our engineer was a man named Chuck. When a major manufacturer he had worked for closed the plant where he worked, he simply started his own business. He was great. His approach was that these issues were only speed bumps and we would find ways around the obstacles.

I remember the water runoff people who wanted us to build a huge retention pond in what would have almost been the front yard. Besides being a safety hazard and a mosquito breeding ground, it would have been incredibly ugly. Chuck suggested a compromise, with a big pipe underground and a smaller pipe leading from the big pipe into the storm water runoff. They agreed, and I am sure it had much to do with Chuck's folksy, down-to-earth approach.

The fire marshal wanted five loud blasters in the six-thousand-square-foot warehouse, which was open wall to wall. If they ever went off, the sound would have resulted in ear damage. Chuck got the regulator to agree to one blaster and one backup.

Our new wheel-chair-accessible handicapped restroom would not pass because we had a mirror over the sinks. We also had installed a full-length mirror that went to the floor on another wall in the restroom, but that didn't count because a person in a wheelchair might not be able to see the mirror that was over the sink. The state inspector said that the law would not allow him to approve the building for occupancy.

Chuck put his arm on the inspector's shoulder and in his real down-to-earth, folksy way asked whether it would be okay to just remove the mirror over the sink. Then everyone could use the same full-length mirror. The inspector thought a moment and then agreed.

We removed the mirror until after the inspector left and put it back up a few weeks later. Chuck was right. The regulators were just speed bumps in the road of progress.

What Driver's License?

*Spot tickets for events that no mere
mortal could expect to get.*

Jim was a great hire for our company. He retired a bit early from what was once Pittsburgh's mighty steel industry. Initially, he had some earning limitations and came to work for us in the permanent part-time category. He quickly became a crew chief for a three-person team at his work site. As the company grew, I needed a part-time supervisor for four similar work sites in the same geographic area, about one and a half hours driving time from most of our other customers.

Jim took the job, and at first we gave him gas money for his personal car. Then, as we added more customers and as the time required for his supervision increased, we increased his pay and provided a vehicle with an expense account.

About two years later, during a driver review for new insurance, Jim had one excuse after another for not giving his driver's license number to the secretary who had to file the report to the insurance company. After a few days of excuses, it was clear something was amiss. I got Jim aside and basically said, "Okay, Jim, come clean. What's up?"

Jim didn't have a driver's license. He had never renewed his license when he came back from military service twenty-eight years before. He had to be a good driver; he was never stopped or issued a ticket in those twenty-eight years.

Jim sat in the office until his wife came to get him, and with my permission, after seeing her license, she drove the company car and acted as Jim's chauffeur until he was issued a license. It might have seemed like an inconvenience for his wife, but she hugged me to death for forcing Jim to get the license. She and his grown children had been on his case for many years.

As the company grew, we added very firm policies about driving. When I think of the trouble we could have gotten into, I am still surprised we didn't cover that base. I suppose it just shows how easily companies can get into trouble.

Jim became one of our area managers, and in addition, he evolved into our company's party specialist. He just took on the job of arranging years of company-wide parties, usually at an amusement park. This gave people from the many different job sites a chance to meet each other and have some fun. I really needed someone to put together such activities and was always thankful for his efforts.

Jim also had ways to get spot tickets for events that no mere mortal could expect to get. He was high up in many organizations such as the Knights of Columbus and the Sierra Club. He was also a zoning commissioner for the county. He once told me that knowing the bishop helped. I do know that, in Pittsburgh, if you want to get tickets for the Pittsburgh Steelers game, you almost have to inherit them. Jim could still get tickets for those games and any special event. This was a benefit of knowing Jim and was enjoyed by many of our employees and customers.

A Moment of Silent Prayer

I can do that.

Really good supervisors have a special way of breaking the rules, keeping the team together, and getting more work done. Such a supervisor had two employees with her when she walked into a room where a very good employee had sat down and fallen asleep. Carol was a very demanding and no-nonsense supervisor. The two employees looked at the supervisor and tensed their faces. I suppose that you could almost hear them thinking, "What is Carol going to do?"

Carol loudly called to the sleeping employee. "Sam," she almost yelled. Sam jumped a little, opened his eyes, and looked straight at Carol. After a moment of awkward silence, Sam said, "What is the matter, Carol? Can't a fellow close his eyes for a moment of silent prayer?"

Now, this could be a real test for a good supervisor. What would you do? Think about it for a moment before you read the next paragraph.

Carol cracked a smile and said, "I can understand the need for prayer for anyone who has a job as hard as the one you do. However, in the future, pray before you start. Then, when you are finished, thank God that you were able to do such great work."

Sam simply said, "I can do that." Carol had avoided the need for a verbal lashing or disciplinary action on an otherwise good employee. Sam avoided being severely embarrassed, and he never again engaged in silent prayer during work hours.

I Wouldn't Hire You on a Bet

Stupid enough to call back.

When our business was still very new, the office was in our home. We had a room allocated for business. I would organize and run the jobs, and my wife would do the bookwork. We had three small children at that time. The youngest was only a few months old, and the next was only fifteen months older than the baby.

The company was starting some new work in a new geographic area, and I had placed a help wanted ad in the local newspaper of that community. The ad also said to call between 8:00 a.m. and 7:00 p.m. When the phone rang at 2:30 one morning, my wife, the babies, and I were startled awake. The caller worked at the newspaper building where I had placed the ad and had seen the early printing being prepared. Over the sound of the now-crying babies, I asked, "Why are you calling now instead of the 8:00 a.m. to 7:00 p.m. listed in the ad?"

He told me that he thought the business phone number might have a call-forwarding feature and he might get someone at home. I said, "Let me see whether I have this straight. You didn't make a mistake reading the ad. You actually thought you could get through to someone's home at 2:30 in the morning." He excitedly replied, "Yeah, yeah, that's right." By this time the babies were crying even louder and my wife was desperately trying to get them back to sleep.

New parents know how absolutely exhausted you can be with new babies. This very tired dad lost his cool and just said, "You damn fool! I wouldn't hire you on a bet," and then

I slammed the phone down. I was really short-tempered, but that fellow was just too much, and I was way too tired. I also took the phone off the hook, just in case he was stupid enough to call back.

Learning to Read

*He almost cried when he
told me he could not continue.*

Our company had such a mix of talent and education. We had several people with PhDs and a few people who were illiterate. The first time it came to my attention that a hard-working and well-spoken twenty-six-year-old could not read, I was shocked. It was hard to believe that a young person couldn't read or write in this modern age. He could write his name and knew a few words, traffic signs, and such, but he could not read a set of instructions.

When discussing the problem with the employee, I discovered that he hadn't been in school since he was eight years old. Helping him learn to read seemed the right thing to do. I offered to set him up with a company that specialized in teaching adults to read. He could attend class after hours, and our company would pay one hundred percent of the cost. He beamed from ear to ear. It was easy to see that he was really excited, and I could put it in the financial books as an investment in a good, hard-working employee.

He missed class the first day he was to start. Then, he missed some of the classes the following week. I called the young man into my office and eyeball-to-eyeball asked, "What is up?" He almost cried when he told me that he could not continue to go to the classes. His wife threatened to leave with their young daughter if he learned to read.

The marital arrangement was exactly the way she liked it. He worked and turned over his paycheck, and she made all the decisions. She was afraid that if he learned to read, she would no longer have complete control.

It seems strange that people can be so self-centered and so selfish as to deny their own spouse a great opportunity. It is a sad story that shows some of the worst of human nature.

Simple Things

Eliminate the simple things before starting on more complicated problems.

I served as a vice chairman of a local chamber of commerce with a fellow who was the manager of a large local mall. After one chamber meeting, he asked whether I could look at his three big automatic scrubbing machines. First, one had failed and then another, and finally, the last machine was working so poorly that it would not pick up the dirty scrub water.

The manager was a really nice fellow, so I said, "Sure, I will look." We went to the mall and opened the equipment room. I turned on the closest machine. The vacuum motor sounded fine, so I pulled off the vacuum hose that went down to the floor squeegee. I put my hand over the hose and felt a strong vacuum.

I loosened the two wing nuts to remove the squeegee that made contact with the floor and placed the squeegee on top of the machine. The squeegee was full of mop fibers, trash, and who knows what. The whole channel was so clogged that the vacuum could hardly pull any water through. You should know that this whole process took less than sixty seconds.

The manager stood there with his mouth hanging open. "You mean this is it?" he said. "This is all that is wrong?" He told me that he had paid for six new vacuum motors, all kinds of seals, and God knows how many hours of labor. He said, "I even sent one man to the factory training school for a week, and that is all that is wrong."

I cleaned the squeegee channel, replaced the squeegee, and backed the machine out into the hall for a test. The machine worked perfectly. The other two machines had the same problem.

This story has a lesson for all of us. We humans often look for complicated solutions. *The problems we deal with often have quite simple solutions.* At the very least, we should eliminate the simple things before we start looking at more complicated solutions.

Lawyer Meltdown

The sergeant major had the last laugh.

This story is worth telling because there are so many lawyer jokes, and so many people like to hear about real lawyers getting the short end of the stick.

A retired Marine Corps sergeant major worked for our company for many years. He was a really great area manager for our growing company. One young lady in his area was real trouble. Her work varied from very good to very poor. Any criticism, even constructive instructions, had her immediately retreating into various defensive modes. She would claim, "You are just picking on me because I am a woman." She was a challenge.

Eventually, she broke our attendance rules and did so after appropriate warnings. We took the opportunity to release her. She applied for welfare. The welfare department made her file for unemployment compensation and directed her to a free attorney. One government agency was creating work for another government agency. Our tax dollars were hard at work supporting both. Wow—what a great system!

She lost the initial claim, but before she received welfare, her attorney had to file an appeal to the referee level. All the rules of evidence applied at this level of judicial review, and she had the burden of proof. During the hearing, her attorney asked one leading question after another. He abused the rules of evidence so badly that the referee's level of irritation was rapidly and visibly increasing.

At this judicial level, an officer of a corporation can act as counsel for the corporation. I was doing so and offered no objections as the attorney continued his abuse of the rules. There really wasn't any reason to object to his questions because his conduct was only irritating the judge and he was not getting the results he wanted. I just played dumb, and the attorney had no idea that I had a very good command of evidentiary law.

The judge admonished the attorney to follow the rules of evidence. But the judge's words had only a minor, temporary effect. The attorney went on for another thirty-five minutes, with the judge becoming more irritated by the minute. When he finally rested his case, the judge turned to me to allow a cross-examination of the witness.

I asked only two questions. The answers were short and terse, but they could not have been better for our case if I had written them myself. My Navy trial experience then cut in and told me to shut up. I could not get a better response with more questions. I told the judge, "No more questions."

The judge turned to me to present our side of the case. I introduced one document into evidence. It took about fifteen seconds. Then I thought for a moment and resisted the temptation to have our two witnesses testify. "We have no further evidence we wish to present," I said. The judge smiled. He knew that I knew we had just won the case and had no reason to introduce anything that might mitigate the claimant's own answers.

The claimant's attorney looked astonished. He jerked himself straight and said, "Wait a minute. I want to cross-examine their two witnesses." I quietly turned to the judge and softly said, "Your Honor, there is nothing to cross;

they offered no testimony." The judge agreed. The attorney seemed baffled. He puffed out his chest and retorted, "Well, then, I will call them as hostile witnesses. I move that they be called now."

I had been quiet while he had so flagrantly abused the rules of evidence. But then it was my turn to have fun. I said, "Your Honor, you know I am not an attorney. However, I seem to recall that unless our two witnesses were to volunteer to testify, they would have to be issued a subpoena some weeks before this hearing." The claimant's attorney looked astonished.

The judge just smiled and asked our two witnesses whether they would choose to be called without a subpoena. They answered an emphatic "No!" The judge glared over toward the abusive attorney and said, "Motion denied." The attorney got really hot, yelling all sorts of objections. The judge threatened a contempt citation and closed the case.

When we were leaving the building and nearing the entrance, we found the abrasive attorney and his client. We were not looking for them, but there they were. That attorney was really hot. He was in a total meltdown. He called us every profanity in the book, plus some I had never heard before—and I had a few years in the Navy.

Our great area manager (the retired Marine Corps sergeant major) just smiled until we were out of the presence of the claimant and her free attorney. Then he started to laugh harder and longer than I ever heard that old marine laugh.

Luck

The part played by luck.

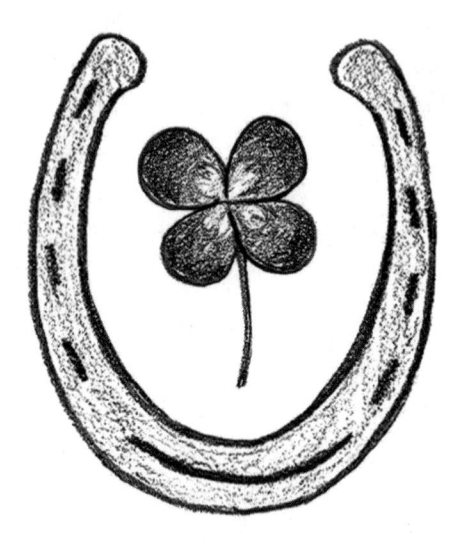

The company was still so new that I was doing all the sales. In an adjacent community, I presented three nice service proposals in the same week. Typically, I could expect to land one new contract for each five proposals that we presented. Our proposal might be fifteen to twenty pages of details of what we would be doing for our customer, as well as the great things about our company, all custom tailored and very professional looking.

Two of the proposals went very well, and I really thought we might get both. The third proposal was for a seventy-thousand-square-foot store. We presented this proposal to a store manager named Abbot who was rather aloof, egotistical, and more than a bit overbearing. It was easy to tell he was not really interested in anything in the proposal.

His body language conveyed his irritation and that he only wanted me to go away. I left after presenting the proposal and thought that the probability of getting this one was just less than zero.

The first two proposals were for two nice executive office buildings. These were one of the classes of customers that I wanted. A lot of extra effort was put into trying to land those two, but no such luck. It would take another twelve years before we got one of these, and we never did get the other one.

It was absolutely poor salesmanship on my part, but I did not make more than one follow-up sales call after presenting the retail proposal. It just seemed a waste of time.

About four weeks later, that same overbearing, egotistical manager called and said, "What do I have to do to start this contract?" That question just about knocked my socks off, and he wanted to start the next morning. I negotiated a start in three days. Because I did not yet have any staff for this location, even three days was going to be a challenge. We started on schedule, with me performing as a frontline supervisor and directing the activities. Abbot was still impatient and terse whenever we spoke.

In about four weeks he softened and began to talk to me like a beer-drinking buddy. It was only then that he confessed the real story of the sudden phone call to start service.

Abbot had backed himself into a corner. His district manager was at his store and, according to Abbot, was "reaming him a new ass" about the state of cleaning in his store. Abbot told me he dodged through the various excuses and tried to explain all that he had been doing to solve the problem. His boss would have none if it, and in the middle of the verbal tongue-lashing, he saw my proposal still on the far corner of his desk. He grabbed my proposal, waved it once, and placed it in front of his district manager.

None of the stores in their chain had ever used a contract cleaning service in the past, but Abbot took the offense. He said that he had been trying everything and even solicited a proposal from a private cleaning service. Abbot admitted to me that all he was doing was trying to get his boss off his back, but that was not what happened.

The district manager was hot! He looked at Abbot and snarled, "Well, is it in your budget?" Abbot nodded, and his district manager all but screamed, "Well, then, do it!" That CYA move left Abbot between the proverbial rock and a hard place. He had absolutely no intention of considering a contract service for cleaning. The first store manager suggesting such a deviation from the corporate policy could be risking his career. But now if he didn't try, his district manager would surely fire him.

Some people would say that was luck. Maybe part of it could be called luck, but if I hadn't produced three proposals that week, our company would not have had this new customer. If you think that was luck, wait until you read what happened next.

Another store manager was visiting at Abbot's store and saw how nice the store now looked. A few months had passed, and Abbot had not been fired for doing something that the corporation had never done before. Abbot couldn't resist telling the visiting manager how wise he was in charting a new course when he set up a cleaning contract and how pleased his district manager was with the results. That was all it took. Wham bam—two weeks later we had our second service contract with another store in this retail chain. These two stores were working well, so I made a sales call at their major headquarters store closer to Pittsburgh.

This store was on two floors and was four to five times larger than either of the two stores that we were cleaning. In short order, we had a contract for this store. Eleven new permanent part-time people working 7:00 to 10:00 a.m. were needed. The trick was to organize the people so that the tasks they performed and the work efforts of each person complemented each other.

My natural analytic thought processes and engineering skills came up with a super-efficient workflow. After the first five apprehensive and tension-filled days, the work flow all came together without me having to direct the activities. I didn't have to be there saying, "Now you do this, and now you go there."

The crew members had learned their parts and understood how they all fit together. It was a beautiful thing to see. Because each part was interconnected, there was a natural drive from each employee to hit his or her mark on time. It provided a hustle that was impressive to behold. I had even worked a site supervisor into the crew.

The store was improving so rapidly that a special enthusiastic pride and sense of camaraderie began to permeate the crew. Such emotions are contagious. I did what I could to foster that pride, but the truth is that the store was getting so much better so fast that everyone could see it. Every new compliment produced even more pride, and that in turn produced a greater effort.

This store was the regional headquarters for the chain. In the early morning during the time our crew was working, management meetings were often held there for all the managers in the region. These managers saw hustle and pride far in excess of anything they had in their stores. In less than one year, our company had contracts for an additional twelve stores.

Was that luck? Did we just accidentally get the right crew? Did that first good job at Abbot's store just naturally lead to the fifteen new retail customers?

If you still believe in luck, let me tell you what happened next. Two years after our company had secured the last store in the geographic region, the chain filed first a Chapter 11 bankruptcy, followed by a full liquidation six months later. That was about fifty percent of our company's sales volume at that time. So much for luck!

Chapter 5:

Government Is Here to Help

An Al Capone Imitation

Justifications for extortion.

Al Capone would have been proud to see the Pennsylvania Human Relations Commission in action. When originally put into operation, the premise was no doubt honorable. I am sure the idea was that a mediation agency with individuals skilled in compromise could find that common ground and cooler heads could prevail. Aggrieved individuals would be better served, and a quicker resolution should be achieved. Thus, a full-blown federal EEOC trial could be avoided. It sounded like a good idea.

So many government programs start with good intentions that become distorted by people expanding their missions. This became a perfect example. Whenever an employee or ex-employee alleged discrimination because of his or her age, race, or sex, the great government commission leaped into action. There was an official call from a Pennsylvania Human Relations individual with an impressive title and intimidating demeanor.

He or she would open with something like, "Could you just give Susie the job back?" or "Give Bob the promotion" or "Give Tom a raise" or whatever the allegedly aggrieved party wanted. If you did not immediately agree, then what I refer to as the employer's penalty phase began.

The agency began by requiring endless volumes of records and reports to be submitted. After the first shipment of reports, we were again asked to give in to whatever the agency wanted. Right or wrong was never an issue. You either gave in or more reports were required. If you thought that you were right and were strong-willed enough not to give in, then a face-to-face hearing was required. This should have been a good thing, but the downside was that the Human Relations Commission individuals were so one sided in their views that objectivity was most often lost. I guess that just came with the job.

This state agency was founded on the idea that it would be doing something positive. It was a really frightening feeling to sit in a hearing and realize that this whole government agency's existence depended on finding discrimination and documenting how it was solving the problem. That was the only way the agency could increase the size of its operation or at least continue to get funding. Just imagine how that helped the officials maintain objectivity.

We went through the ordeal nine times over three decades, although only four people were involved. One person could make multiple filings. The attempted extortion was so bad that an official would call (never write) and say that if I would agree to give the claimant X amount of money, the complaint would be withdrawn; otherwise, more reports would be required.

Al Capone would have loved these folks. There is very little difference between "Sell my beer or I wreck your establishment" and what these people were doing, except perhaps that they wrapped themselves in a feeling of moral superiority, convinced that they were doing something good.

I often wonder whether "Big Al's" men also came up with altruistic justifications for their extortion methods.

I Owe How Much?

More turns than a bucket of worms.

The company had reached a sales volume that was large enough to attract an audit that took several days for the state sales tax department. I am afraid to think what would have happened if all the books had not been so meticulously kept, completely accurate, and fully computerized.

When the audit was finished, I was handed a paper with the results. It read that we were to pay the Commonwealth of Pennsylvania one hundred and twenty-seven thousand dollars. "You want one hundred and twenty-seven thousand dollars for sales or use tax!" I gasped. All I could think was "Good God, where did that come from?" A heart attack would probably have been in order, but I just got mad. I was not angry-mad, just upset-mad. Just imagine how you would feel if some state official came to your business and told you that you owed the state that much money when you thought that everything was being done perfectly.

I called our accounting firm that had a reputation for excellence. It quickly pointed out some serious errors by the state, but much remained; one hundred and twenty-seven thousand was a big number. We had to get copies of the law and study the case precedents. The sales tax laws in the state of Pennsylvania have more turns than a bucket of worms.

We had to put the business growth on hold and prepare our answers because the audit provided only a limited time frame for a response. After a couple of weeks of intense study and recalculation on our part, we determined that instead of owing the state one hundred and twenty-seven thousand dollars, we had actually overpaid by almost twenty thousand dollars, based on the proper application of the law.

We scheduled our resolution conference. The state auditor brought his boss. I took them to a conference room and skipped the coffee. This was serious, and I was loaded for bear. We had a company team effort, with each person firing a barrel before the next hit and then firing another barrel again. We scarcely gave time for a response. We took almost all morning while our accounting team and company officers quoted the law. I handed them the case precedents from the courts and introduced whole new topics showing tax we had given the state that should not have been collected.

When we were done, silence filled the room. Not a sound was heard for what seemed like an eternity, until I said, "How would you guys like some coffee?" Not a chair moved, and they just looked at each other. They were dazed and looked like deer in headlights.

They had a problem. The state employed them to collect money, not to give it back. When the day was done, we agreed to call it a wash. I got nothing back and they collected nothing, but they did go away.

They came back about five years later and spent almost a whole week and could find only that one company we had ordered from had forgotten to include the sales and usage tax on just a few of its invoices. We had not noticed because these were minor items not involved with resale. The total overlooked sales tax was about one hundred and ten dollars. We paid it, and they went away. Because they had devoted so much audit time for such a measly return, the auditor shook his head and commented, "We'll probably never see the sales tax people again."

I only wish that were so. The third and last audit is a story so egregious in concept it bears a separate telling.

You Are Not Employees Anymore

No precedent for the record.

Some years ago, the Pennsylvania legislative body wanted more money and passed a sales tax on services. Of course, the tax did not apply to the richer and more politically connected types of service business and certainly did not apply to major campaign contributors. Janitorial companies had to collect sales tax. Bill-collecting companies had to collect sales tax, but attorneys collecting billing did not have to collect sales tax on their services.

It is important to understand that businesses do not really pay taxes. They do collect a lot of money for the various taxing groups, but that cost is always added to the cost of their product or service. After the tax on services was passed, the large property management companies in the Philadelphia area came together and threatened to quit supporting the political establishment without some relief from the tax that was now included in the service bill to them. They added it to the cost of their rent, but that made their rents higher than in New Jersey, just over the river.

Now, these people had some clout, so the legislature passed a change in the law that allowed employee wages, payroll taxes, and other employee-related expenses to be exempt from the calculations. What was left were essentially supplies, equipment, most operating costs, overhead, and budget profits. Of course, actual profits were taxed again via the corporate net income tax.

Remember from the previous tale that Pennsylvania sales tax laws have more curves than a bucket of worms.

Many years later, the state sales tax department came up with a "revenue-enhancing" idea (its actual words) to increase money collected by the state.

The department decided that executives, managers, supervisors, office workers, and sales personnel would no longer be considered employees. All the wages, payroll tax, and benefits paid to these employees would no longer be exempt from the state sales tax. The state sales tax people started to collect current taxes and retroactive taxes for the previous three years. They had already collected from lots of companies before they got to us. They decided they wanted seventy-six thousand dollars, which included some interest and penalties for underpayment based on the agency's new creative interpretation that some employees were not actually employees. Naturally, they also applied this new interpretation retroactively.

The auditor left his report for us to check and scheduled a return visit with his supervisor because of the high dollar amount. The return visit made for an interesting meeting. They just assumed we would pay up and nicely offered time payments with interest. The time payments were for our ease of payment.

Now I ask if you don't think that wasn't so nice of them. Put yourself in that situation: a brand-new interpretation of existing policy and they wanted it applied retroactively.

When I replied to the two of them, I was very nice. I was also very polite, but an earthy translation of my reply would have been "Go to hell!" We started the appeal process and hoped for the best. I thought that if we could give them an excuse to find in our favor, we could put an end to the nonsense. We had excellent facts on our side.

There were zero case precedents involving our industry. We had a letter from the secretary of the taxation department on letterhead with an example of the proper application of the sales tax on service. We had received this letter in response to a question I had posed when the employee exemption law was first passed. We were doing the sales tax exactly as outlined by the previous administration's top dog for taxes.

We had a number of other factors operating in our favor, including transcripts of the legislative debate during the passing of this particular law that clearly showed the intent of the legislative body. I hoped we could simply use one or more of those and they would back off. But the possibility of extracting money from their newly created interpretations of the law was too strong.

Some wise person once said the art of taxation was getting the maximum amount possible without actually killing the host. I suppose that thinking of government as a parasite is not that far off. Actually, I know we need government, and there are many good things government can do, but I am equally confident that we don't need all the government we pay for.

The first two levels of our appeal were unsuccessful. However, I was still confident we would prevail when we got out of the department of taxation appeal system and into commonwealth court. We would demand a jury trial. There was nothing hard to understand about our case. Imagine what real people would think about paying three years of back taxes for violating a law that didn't exist at the time and, for that matter, that still did not exist.

I was confidant that while the state may huff and puff, it could not actually allow the case to get to court. You really do not have to be that smart to understand what a jury would most likely decide. In court, if we lost, the state would get its seventy-six thousand dollars and a bit more interest. If it lost, it would have to return tens of millions of dollars it had already collected or was about to collect from multiple companies. Even if the state were to appeal, it would have to stop collecting while it was appealing.

The state tax people simply could not let a real court establish a precedent that would stop the collections for their new revenue enhancement idea. The state held out longer than I thought it would. It rejected our arguments and told us we would have to pay even more. A bit later it offered a lesser payment as a compromise.

Entrepreneurial business owners can be strong-willed risk takers. I was still thinking the original "Go to hell." I turned it down. This was going to be all or nothing. Being right was far more important than the seventy-six thousand dollars.

About a year after the last contact from the tax appeal system, we received a letter from the state attorney general. The state sales tax people found a creative way to get themselves off the hook. When it became apparent we could not be manipulated, they referred the case to the state attorney general, who decided not to go forth. The attorney general provided a special ruling for our company that exempted our company but only our company.

No court precedent was established, and the state could continue to collect taxes from my competitors. Furthermore, I was also not supposed to tell others! By the time we had the final resolution, I had sold the company and started semiretirement. Because we had made a stock sale, the purchasing company retained this competitive advantage.

Three Philadelphia Lawyers

Blinding prejudice can obscure the truth.

Federal wage and hour people are not really malevolent. They just come from an environment so separated from reality that they are unable to see what should have been apparent to any unbiased individual. It all started when a federal wage and hour employee called for an appointment to examine a host of records.

A grumpy, stone-faced individual arrived at the appointed time and looked through reams of records, all of which were in perfect order. Even all the I-9 immigration forms had the appropriate document numbers and signatures. She left, after a day of tying up three or four of our people's time that could have been spent doing something to build the business.

If I remember correctly, she returned a few weeks later with a brilliant idea that we should pay four people about nine hundred dollars. Two were past employees who had been let go for poor performance. Two were current employees. One current employee was a nephew of one of the first two, and the other current employee was a neighbor.

Without going into all the details of proper time-reporting procedures for payroll, let me assure you that any reasonable person would have found no merit to the claims. I was confident that when a supervisor reviewed the material, the truth would easily be seen. That didn't happen. Eventually, the matter proceeded until the government assigned an attorney to the complaint.

When an attorney was first assigned, I thought that was great. Now, a bright, objective, and unbiased person would be examining the records and statements. I was sure that when the government wage and hour attorney actually looked at the records, the truth would be so obvious that we would just shake hands and he or she would go home. How naive I was and how much I still had to learn.

One employee later volunteered that he signed the complaint only to please his ex-employee uncle, and he told the wage and hour attorneys that. The other current employee later complained that he tried to withdraw after the case started, even telling the federal attorney, "It wasn't really like that." He alleged that he was told he had to stay with his original statement or he would be guilty of a crime and would be prosecuted for having made false official statements.

It seemed to me that the environment in which the wage and hour people worked was so biased that their instinctive reaction was always to see an employer as an evil scoundrel who was abusing poor, innocent employees. So distorted was their frame of mind that it appeared they actually believed we were doing something wrong, although all tangible evidence showed the exact opposite.

They seemed sure that all employers abused people and that some just hid it better than others. Even an original party to the claim who told them they were wrong was not good enough to open their eyes. They probably thought he was just scared.

We eventually went to federal court. The wage and hour people started out wanting only nine hundred dollars. We would be paying an attorney that much, so what was the point of going to trial? It was a stupid sense of what was right and what was wrong that steeled my determination to do what was right.

The wage and hour people wouldn't let two of the people drop the complaint and paid all four people's expenses and their wages to come to court. I remember thinking, "My taxes are hard at work again." The government did not offer to pay my wages or the wages of our twelve other witnesses. Of course, I didn't expect it to do so. (I just want to take a writer's prerogative to reflect on the concept of fair play.)

Nevertheless, the government did make one change. It upped its claim to thirty-nine thousand dollars. It seemed that the law allowed the government to add on all the expenses of its staff attorneys: their plane trips, hotels, meals, and other expenses. Given this kind of leverage, it is a minor miracle that the wage and hour people ever lose a case.

It is important to remember that when the wage and hour people do win, that is far from meaning they were right. It most often means that people wiser than me simply pay to get them to go away so that the business can get back to what is important. But I was too far down the road when I came to realize that the wage and hour people were simply unable to see the truth.

We prepared well for this case. My old Navy law school training and duty as trial counsel were valuable beyond words. Our witnesses were well prepared. I had written direct testimony questions for each, with probable cross-examination questions that would come from the wage and hour attorneys. We practiced and practiced. I taught people to avoid rambling when answering cross-examination questions a nd to stick only to facts we needed. We practiced giving information on a cross-exam that would be impossible to get into the record via direct questioning from our attorney.

We practiced how to answer and how to give our attorney time to object.

Our attorney interviewed our witnesses and was astonished at their smooth, professional answers. He tried some imaginative cross and found people well prepared and at ease. He made a few minor changes in my brief, and we went to trial. We were in federal court in downtown Pittsburgh for one and a half days. At the conclusion, we won everything.

The judge said, "The testimony of the government's six plaintiffs was inconsistent, contradictory, and at times self-contradictory, nor were the government's allegations supported by the documentary evidence in the case." I could provide you with three pages of other direct quotes. The judge lectured the government's three Philadelphia lawyers for fifteen minutes about the improprieties of their case. They deserved that lecture and much more.

Even after the strong scolding by the judge, the wage and hour people sent us a letter saying they were going to appeal and it would cost us even more money. (Their big stick was broken, and they were now reaching for an even bigger stick.) With all my testosterone on the line, I countered, "Go ahead and have at it."

I then provided a reference to a little-known law that allows companies to collect triple damages when the government abuses its power. I told them it appeared that the law was intended for exactly this situation and to appeal if they wished. If it had been a poker game, I would have just matched the bet and tripled the stakes.

A day or so later, they withdrew the threat of an appeal without any comment. Perhaps some higher-up actually read the case and discovered how wrong they had been from the very beginning, but probably not. Their natural bias would have made it hard for them to see the truth.

What likely happened was that someone decided that they just might lose and they should not again underestimate our ability to present a compelling case.

When the case first went to federal court, you will remember that two people in the case were still working for our company. As a footnote, let me tell you that of the two, one quit six years later because of medical problems, and the other was still working when I sold the company. Some thirteen-plus years had passed, and he told me several times how embarrassed he was when the wage and hour attorneys threatened him with prosecution if he changed his story and told the truth. So blinding was the government's prejudice that it had obscured the obvious truth.

I opened this story with the statement that the federal wage and hour people were not really malevolent. Still, it is truly sad and also scary how some people in authority can become so myopic as to be incapable of seeing the obvious.

We Found a New Job for You

We were wasting our time and dollars.

All states have unemployment compensation systems that are in general conformance with federal law. Most states added a job placement service. The original purpose was to help those unemployed people who registered for benefits to find new jobs. Like most government programs, that mission expanded, and soon it became a general employment service in competition with the commercial employment services.

The state encouraged people to sign up for its placement services and encouraged employers to use the state service. Two big advantages for an employer were no placement fees and a prescreening process. An employer could identify the skills or abilities it was looking for and let the state screen out those who did not meet the criteria. Such a process was a great help to the employer in avoiding spurious legal challenges in employee hiring. There was always the potential lawsuit about why you hired Sally instead of Mary. If Mary obtained the services of a contingent fee attorney who demanded a monetary settlement, that attorney would then have to sue the state.

As many people know, the state can simply declare itself exempt. The legal concept is a holdover from old English law, where the king was always right.

This hiring practice seemed attractive, so I decided to try it where we were starting work in a new and remote geographic location. The state service told me that it did not have much of a reserve to call on for our permanent part-time janitorial service jobs. It suggested that I run help wanted ads using the phone number at its office. It would then do the screening and set up interviews for me. That sounded like a good approach. I did my part and placed the ads.

Only six people showed up for an interview, and I hired four. When they arrived, the state had the people fill out a form to make sure it would get credit for the hire. That was to be expected. What I did not yet know was that one of the forms asked whether job candidates would like the state job service to call them if another job became available that had higher pay, benefits, or more hours. Only a fool would have said no to that question.

About three weeks after starting our new contract, the state job service did call one of our new employees and arranged for him to interview for a much-better-paying job. The employee quit. He was gone, and our three weeks of training went with him. I didn't blame the employee. The offer was too good. However, I did not use the state job service again.

It didn't make sense to spend our company advertising dollars that then provided the state with prospects to call for another job. I know that this is not really germane to the story, but I often wondered whether the state got credit for two hires in such a situation.

The Roads Are Closed

A different perspective.

The governor decided a blizzard was so bad that he officially closed the roads. Only emergency vehicles were to be out and about. About a week later, during a news interview, the governor expressed surprise that most businesses didn't pay people for the missed day, as the government had.

I wrote to the governor and also editorialized in the papers that the governor was absolutely right. But because businesses didn't earn any money with which to pay the people who did not work, we needed a tax rebate for the monies not earned so we could pay the people who did not work. I was sure that when it became an issue of reducing state income, the governor would have a whole different perspective.

I wasn't expecting him to do anything about my suggestion, and I tell this story only to show how differently the government and free enterprise view the same set of facts. I also wondered why he didn't suggest that most employees could use a personal day or make up the missed time later.

OSHA Wants What?

God, save us from such foolish regulators.

When the Occupational Safety and Health Administration (OSHA) was new, it would inspect buildings and make such silly rulings that it badly tarnished its image; just the mention of OSHA would cause either laughter or tears in the business community. My first encounter involved an inspector at an industrial manufacturing plant that was a customer of our janitorial service company.

I remember a citation for restroom partitions not having the proper opening from the floor to the bottom of the partitions. I remember that our customer had to move all the restroom partitions one and a half inches. A year later, no one could remember whether they needed to be moved up or down that one and a half inches.

The ceiling of the warehouse was twenty-four feet to the overhead ceiling lights. We used a fiberglass-insulated telescoping pole with a suction grip on the end to efficiently remove the burned-out bulbs and then to install new bulbs. OSHA ruled that all overhead lightbulbs had to have guards installed to keep employees from bumping their heads into the lightbulbs and electrocuting themselves.

There were no twenty-four-foot-tall people working in that factory. Nothing in the plant came anywhere close to that height. Unmoved by logic, OSHA still would not hear of an exception to its rule. The company had to install guards over the bulbs and then buy a special high-lift to get to the guard to remove it and then change a light. It should have been obvious that this introduced far more hazards, but this was a government rule, so it had to be followed to avoid a fine.

I often wondered what it was about the regulatory mindset that could not see through such foolishness. The good news is that OSHA was so aggressive in foolish applications that a business and legislative rebellion introduced more reasonable applications over time.

Regulatory agencies often perform a needed function. However, they will always require citizens' attention. They naturally tend to become dictatorial, with an attitude that they are always right. They are always sure that they know so much better than everyone else what is good for you and me and the rest of society. May God save us all from such foolish regulators.

Nonprofit

How can we really help?

Competition from nonprofit groups is a sore point with almost every businessperson that I know. It is not politically correct to criticize nonprofit organizations. However, I have never been all that politically correct, so I will tell the tale anyway and hope some good comes from the telling.

Nonprofit organizations don't pay taxes on their property, supplies, equipment, etc., and they don't have to charge their customers sales tax. Yet they still compete with real tax-paying businesses. That certainly is a handicap for a business to overcome. But the good news for business and our whole economic system is that as competitors, they are generally pretty poor, at least in our janitorial services industry. Because they are so bad and because it sounds so nice to help handicapped nonprofits or similar groups, government comes to the rescue.

One such state attempt involved the state's own service work. The state would ask for a sealed competitive bid to perform services at a state facility. When the bids were opened and the lowest—or sometimes the most responsible—bid was identified, guess what happened? If you think that the low bid would get the job, you have to guess again. That did not happen in the state of Pennsylvania. The state turned to the representative of the nonprofit lobby in the state capital, and any organization under the nonprofit umbrella that wanted to match the dollar bid got the award. When the contract was awarded to a group such as the blind, there would have been some justice if only the blind really did clean the state government offices.

That is not what really happened. The nonprofit groups hired mostly nonhandicapped individuals, and the contract was simply a way to raise money. As more and more businesses refused to participate in the charade, the few remaining bids would get higher and higher. Sometimes they were even high enough for the very unprofessional nonprofit group to actually do a credible job.

The lawmakers never seemed to consider that if the state contract simply required a successful contractor to hire handicapped individuals directly, a huge positive could be achieved. The state could save large sums of money, and the handicapped individuals would be working in a real work environment with a real tax-paying business. This could also provide opportunities for growth and advancement for such individuals. In some states, handicapped groups and businesses can work together because their state laws encourage such actions, but not in Pennsylvania.

I remember thinking that legislators would understand the problem if after winning a hard-fought election their seat was offered to any handicapped group agreeing to accept the same pay. I know that is just a fun fantasy, but it does put the problem in perspective. Our state's present system has much room for improvement.

I remember calling a local agency that supported the handicapped when we were starting service for a new customer and needed about twenty-two new people. One section of that customer's facility had an opening for a four-hour shift of five people doing nonskilled and very repetitive tasks. Some handicapped individuals cannot work a shift as long as eight hours, so the four-hour shift would have been great. Five people for a short four-hour shift, all in sight of each other and easily supervised, seemed a natural employment opportunity for special people in a handicapped group.

This should have been a really great opportunity to do some good and help, so I called a local agency. The answer I got was "No, we can't let our people go. We might get a contract to assemble some boxes here at our sheltered center." How sad that they didn't understand that the goal should have been to get people into society, not to retain a permanent handicapped workforce.

Just in case you are feeling comfortable because your state has a better system, let me tell you that the federal government has an even more egregious program. A federal agency for the handicapped simply reviews existing contracts and then decides which ones they want. The contracts are awarded to the group and forever taken out of the free-enterprise market. Generous yearly increases are awarded, and never again are free competitions required. Again, if the government really wanted to help, it would simply require a contractor to have handicapped participation and it could easily verify the results via Social Security numbers. This would require very few regulatory checks (which is a proper role of government) and would facilitate cooperation with agencies dedicated to helping the handicapped. But, unfortunately, this federal program is more about self-aggrandizement for the groups with a bureaucracy dedicated to showing how much they are doing.

I remember a fellow contractor who lost a contract he had successfully retained for over a decade and who actually employed a few handicapped individuals. (I specifically remember one with Down syndrome.) The federal group claimed the contract. The officials came to the site and offered jobs to all the people who were already working there.

All that immediately changed was the checks came from the new non-tax-paying entity and about forty percent of the previous employees were now classified as handicapped. People taking medication to regulate blood sugar, people who were hard of hearing, and those with arthritis were now classified as handicapped. It must have looked impressive on the records. Too bad they didn't have a truth-in-disclosure statement revealing that these were the same people who had already been working at that facility and most had not previously considered themselves as handicapped.

Common Sense

We can't issue an occupancy permit.

Our company was in the last stages of a seven-thousand-square-foot expansion of office and warehouse space. In the process, we added a large restroom that would serve as a handicap restroom and a modernized ladies' restroom. We had placed a large mirror over the sinks as well as a full-length mirror on an adjacent wall. A building inspection was required prior to issuing an occupancy permit. The inspector informed me that he could not approve our building. I almost fell off the chair. "What is wrong?" I asked. He explained that a handicapped individual in a wheelchair would not be able to see the mirror over the sinks. Such a mirror denied equal access, even with the full-length mirror on the adjacent wall.

I didn't know whether I should laugh or cry. Knowing that such regulators would take serious offense at a smart reply, I bit my lip and played the game. I said something like, "Oh, my, what can we do? Another mirror under the sink does not seem practical."

The man who designed the expansion project was a very talented and down-home type of engineer. He "ah-shucked" the inspector a bit and asked whether we could just take down the mirrors. The inspector thought for a moment and volunteered that if we didn't have a mirror over the sinks, then there would be equal access and he could sign off on the inspection.

I JUST KNOW THERE'S A MIRROR IN HERE SOMEWHERE!

Our shop repair department had the mirrors off the wall in about four minutes. The inspector signed off, and we waited almost two weeks before we put the mirrors back, just to make sure he did not come back.

Sometimes it seems that the regulatory community is frightfully slow to apply common sense. I suppose it is like the airport screeners searching an eighty-year-old grandmother traveling with her family while letting others through to avoid profiling too many people from one group. Well, the good news is that they seem to learn even if it does take far too long.

Chapter 6:

Management—
Good, Bad, and Ugly

Not Me! Where Can I Hide?

Drive the train; don't be a passenger.

"Not me! Where can I hide?" seemed to be the attitude of some people in larger companies that were downsizing. Some of our customers' people were often at a loss for what to do. Some people just tried to hide or to get below the radar screen. Sometimes they were close to retirement or a pension and were simply afraid for their job.

In most cases they were the ones who followed along but never made the company work. They were much like passengers on a train. If the train had problems and was slowing or stopping, they didn't know what to do. They often were successful yes-people who could look busy but never contributed to making the company better than the competition.

The good and aggressive employees, who still had careers to build or "mountains to climb," often found opportunities elsewhere during a downsizing. The problem was that companies too often promoted mediocrity. Unlike the military, they failed to thin the ranks as people moved up, keeping only the best of the best.

In a specific case that comes to mind, our company had just been awarded a three-year service contract in a downtown metropolitan area, for two office buildings totaling over one million square feet and forty-two stories. The customer was downsizing, as technology decreased the need for what once was a labor-intensive business, and it desperately needed to reduce costs. When downsizing, it was reducing cleaning specifications at the same time. As an example, vacuuming carpets in office areas was reduced from daily to only once per week in the new competitive environment. This decrease in cleaning specifications was a top management goal, and top management was right. It needed to be done.

Remember that this was a new contract for our company, and you should know that the previous service company was a large contractor with operations all over the United States, but there they had performed rather poorly. The customer's employees in the building were upset. They had written nasty letters to the CEO, and the union had already filed several grievances.

We came in as a new contractor with greatly reduced cleaning specifications and employees that were already hostile. Before you think I must have been nuts to tackle this job, I ask you to consider the possibilities. We were a growing suburban company with an opportunity to establish our footprint in a major metropolitan area. It would also give us major high-rise office building service contracts with a Fortune 500 company.

I was too aggressive, too stubborn, or too stupid not to try. Businesses have to challenge the future to grow and become better. The first two weeks were hell for us. Our direct contact was the customer's building services manager, and he was in hopelessly over his head. As an example, the employees would complain that no one had vacuumed their office for several days. The building services manager would fax us a "CYA" note telling us the job wasn't getting done. We would point out that we were not supposed to vacuum daily, and he would agree. You would think that would be the end of the problem.

Then the next day, when another employee complained, he would send us another "CYA" note, with a copy to the out-of-state corporate purchasing department. The building services manager would agree with us but would do nothing except hide and hope nothing bad would happen to him.

Finally, the out-of-state purchasing department sent us a formal "get it fixed or else" letter. We were in danger of losing our largest and newest contract. We were doing exactly what the customer's top management wanted, but no one in middle or lower management was willing to take charge or take ownership and move ahead. They were the passengers on that train, just hoping they didn't get thrown off, trying ever so hard to provide cover for themselves.

After several weeks of this, we were in deep manure, and it was clear we needed some dramatic action—and that action wasn't going to come from our customer's building services department. I twisted the arm of the customer's building services manager to allow me to directly contact the customer's department heads and supervisors throughout the buildings.

Previously, we had not been allowed direct contact. He surely would have turned me down if he knew what I had in mind. But I did get the okay—and with enough witnesses to prevent a later change in the story.

I intended to take very forceful action. I was going to open the throttle and drive that train. We might lose the contract, but we were surely going to lose it if I waited for that professional passenger to take any action.

The next morning, I had six very good people go through the buildings with probably a hundred copies of the specifications. We talked to each and every department head and supervisor and anyone else who paused to listen. We talked about their company's need to be fiercely competitive in a deregulated era.

We gave out copies of specifications. We told supervisors which days of the week their area would get a detailed cleaning, including the vacuuming, which wasn't going to happen daily (except in emergencies). We again emphasized how important it would be to help the company be successful for the sake of all their jobs.

The building services manager, who was our immediate contact, was at another building that morning. We started what was an education, motivation, and information crusade. By noontime, the deed was done. Our building services contact arrived at about 1:00 in the afternoon and was terrified. He wasn't mad; he was way too scared to be mad. He was stuttering over his words and sweating like it was a Fourth of July picnic. After the first one and a half hours, he got sick and left for home. A couple of his contemporaries and his boss could only say, "Oh, my God." But it was too late for second-guessing. The deed was done! And then there was silence.

The next day there was not a single complaint all morning. The building services manager's boss was almost in shock. He said he could not believe the phone did not ring off the hook. We knew the phone worked because we had a few requests for specialized services, such as cleaning up someone's coffee spill.

The following day, three employees of the customer called with bogus complaints. These were complaints about things that we were not supposed to be doing. Because we now had access to the customer's supervisors, we went to the supervisors for those three employees.

They shut it down faster than a college bar during a liquor raid. In a matter of two days, we went from about sixty nasty complaints per day to almost none. The third day, the building services manager got well and came back to work. He jumped right into taking credit for "getting us squared away." It was almost sad to hear because so many people already knew exactly what had happened. It wasn't even a creditable claim. He lasted a few more months and then was transferred to something else for a few more months until he left the company.

Opportunity Knocks

Say "yes" when you hear opportunity knocking.

Opportunity knocks and sometimes almost beats your door down. Our first out-of-state customer was just such a case. A retail manager from a local store transferred to another location in a state six hours driving time away. After a couple of months, he called me for help. He asked whether I could give him a proposal for his store. Not a chance, I said in much nicer words and instead offered to help him select a good company in his local area.

A month later, he again asked me to service his store, and again I begged out for what I thought were a lot of good reasons. After another month or two, he called a third time, and after a brief exchange of pleasantries, he said, "I want to put my regional vice president on the line."

I had met this man once and knew his reputation as a no-nonsense type of individual. He started out saying, "Chuck, how many stores do you do for us now?" "About sixteen," I answered. After a moment of silence, no doubt for dramatic effect, he said, "I need your company's service here in this store, and I need it now. I want you to understand how serious I am about this. I hope I am real clear?" "Oh, yes, sir," I said. "Good," he replied, "here is Mr. Branner" (store manager). I said, "Mr. Branner, when do you want us to start?" ASAP was his reply. "Is next Monday okay for you?" I asked. I had no idea how we were going to pull this off, but the following Monday we were there.

Our account in the new state wasn't nearly as hard as I thought it would be. A great lesson was learned! That lesson was simply to *say "yes" whenever you hear opportunity knock and figure it out later if you must.*

After that, and as the company grew, we more or less jumped whenever opportunity was there. We once started services simultaneously in twenty separate locations. We ended up adding landscaping service, snow removal service, window cleaning, and mechanical maintenance to what we were already doing. Sometimes our management staff would grab their hearts, get wobbly in the knees, and say, "We are going to do what?" But we did those new things because opportunity does not always knock three times.

Gestapo Mentality

They caught Jesse James.

Gestapo mentality is what comes to mind when I think of one incident in a Service Merchandise store. (I can use the name because the whole chain closed in bankruptcy.) Our two early-morning part-time employees had finished cleaning and clocked out. They were leaving the store when the store manager asked whether they would do a favor for him and take the large wheeled cart of broken toys from the stockroom to the outside Dumpster.

These two were retired, on pension, and really good-natured fellows. They thought the job was fun. It got them out of the house, and they made a little extra money. Actually, I believe their wives liked having them out even more than they liked the excuse to get out, but that is another story.

When these two really great guys started to empty the trash cart into the Dumpster, it was apparent the toys were not beyond repair, so they loaded them in the trunks of their cars and took them to the Marine Corps Toys for Tots location. The marines would then fix the toys and donate them to needy children at Christmas.

Our two employees came into the store the next morning and proudly told everyone the really nice thing they had done. When the store security guards heard what happened, they grilled the two like the Gestapo. After a half hour of questions that could be called intensive interrogation, they sent the two out of the store, called me, and told me they were barred from the store. The store manager could do nothing. The store security was a separate department with a separate reporting structure.

The problem was that the store received credit for damaged merchandise, and the manufacturer did not incur return shipping expenses on assurances from the retailer that the damaged merchandise would be destroyed. Such a policy made sense, but no one on the cleaning team (including me) had ever heard of such a policy before.

I tried to talk to the security supervisor, but a brick wall would have been more receptive. It was as if the security guards had just caught Jessie James. How sad that authority had so warped their common sense. I am sure many of us have seen similar nonsensical abuse by individuals given authority. It is an excellent reason our society always needs a review and appeal process. Such stupidity can upset me, so I wrote to the CEO of the company. CEOs have enough smarts to see such actions as blind stupidity.

The security guards were reprimanded. After that, they really disliked seeing me in the store. About a year later, both were dismissed for unknown reasons. I personally think they were caught with their hands in the cookie jar.

The story does end well. I transferred the two men to another location where they were appreciated and loved almost like family. They told their story for about ten years until the offending store disappeared in bankruptcy.

Cutting Rags for Workers' Compensation

Okay, we will get a bed.

Our company gradually evolved a very aggressive and very effective workers' compensation program. We had a great experience modification factor (.508), which meant we paid about one-half what the average company paid for workers' compensation insurance. With a payroll involving many millions of dollars, this reduction in workers' compensation insurance cost was enough to allow our company to underprice the competition. We could even buy a competitor and immediately start recovering the purchase price with the savings from the workers' compensation insurance cost.

Our aggressive approach began with a single employee named Anna. Anna told some very unkind tall tales about two fellow employees. They got mad, and after a verbal exchange, one of the employees called an area supervisor who was not at the work site.

Because the two employees were leaving the building when the verbal exchange started, the supervisor simply told all of them to go home and cool off. He would be at the site the next evening at the start of the shift.

Can you guess who didn't show up? Anna called off sick about two hours before her shift was scheduled to start. Not just the next day and the day after that but for four days she was too sick to come to work (translation: to face the music).

She then decided to go to Dr. Quack. (You can probably guess that this is a made-up name.) Dr. Quack was very well known locally. Everyone knew him as Eight-Day Quack. He automatically gave anyone a work excuse for eight days. The work excuse forms were even preprinted for the eight days. At that time in Pennsylvania, when employees were off work with a work-related injury, they could often receive full, or sometimes more than full, pay for missed time. However, they had to be off for at least eight days. Anna could get paid to stay home, and Dr. Quack could get a patient visit once or twice a week with premium billing to the workers' compensation fund.

Being sick was not a work-related injury. So guess what happened? Anna reported that she bumped her toe into a file cabinet her last night on the job. The toe was swollen, and she would have to be off until the eighth day. During a chargeable patient visit on the eighth day, Dr. Quack discovered Anna had really injured her knee when she allegedly slipped on ice in the parking lot two weeks before.

We should have known that something more nebulous than a swollen toe was going to be needed to keep up this charade. Now Dr. Quack could continue to bill the workers' compensation insurance carrier, and Anna could continue to collect full pay. The injury did not stop her from making trips to the mall, the grocery store, and sports events. What would you think when confronted with such an obvious fake?

Eventually, we forced a hearing before a workers' compensation administrative law judge. At the hearing, we presented an available light-duty job at our office that we had created just for this purpose. She could cut big rags into smaller rags. The hearing was comical. Her attorney would lead her to say that she needed lots of breaks. We replied, "Sure, no problem." Her attorney would say she might get really tired and have to lie down. We said, "Okay, we will get a bed!" The objections and qualifications went on for about thirty minutes. Eventually, they ran out of excuses, and the judge ordered her to return to work and suspended the wage replacement benefits.

We had her report from 10:00 a.m. to 2:00 p.m. This was a four-hour shift, as she had worked before, but now in the middle of the day. That time schedule really cut into trips to the mall and daytime soaps. Anna worked nine days and then called off. She didn't show the next day or the next.

We called her home and left a message on her answering machine. Still there was no reply. We then sent a letter telling her how important her job was and that we could keep it open only until the end of the next week without some communication from her. We prayed, and our prayers were answered. She did not call. She also did not call the following week or the week after that.

About two months later, we had a call from Anna's new attorney. It seemed that an automobile had hit her back bumper, and she was suffering terrible, terrible pain from whiplash. The attorney wanted to know what she made per week. I told him nothing; she had quit. He wasn't going to give up that easily. He insisted that I send him a letter saying what she earned—and leave out the part about quitting. Now what do you think should have been an appropriate response?

I said "No! Subpoena me for direct testimony." I never heard from him again, and a year later, I heard that Anna was suing someone else.

Once you have to deal with such obvious fraud, you learn to deal with all workers' compensation claims quickly and aggressively. Fortunately, people like Anna are the exceptions.

Never Believe a Salesperson

Try only to convince him or her that you believe.

When I first got out of the U.S. Navy, I went to work for a Philadelphia-headquartered company that was very big in food service at schools, colleges, and hospitals. It had the continental United States divided into nine sales areas, with a very professional sales representative in each area. The company was beginning to market janitorial or housekeeping services to expand its food service operation.

I would go with the sales representative when there was a need to analyze a potential customer's operation to prepare a formal proposal. I anxiously waited until there was an opportunity to go with Russ. Russ sold five times what the other eight salespeople sold. What was his magic?

Think about the opportunity to learn the sales secrets from a star that so far outshined the other very excellent salespeople. Russ told me exactly what he did and how he did it. His first lesson was that *prospective customers never really believe a salesperson.* What the salesperson needs to do is not try to convince the prospects about the value or merits of the service but *try only to convince them that he or she believes.* It is a very subtle difference, but it is most important. When you try to impose your will or force prospects to see the value or merits of your service, they naturally resist or put up walls. When you present yourself as a believer and even show something that brings value to the program, you are not threatening change; you are only showing enthusiasm.

The second major lesson was always to *prequalify the price*. Let's look at the problem using the analogy of a new car. A potential car buyer describes the car he or she would like. It is a fully loaded, top-of-the-line Cadillac, but the problem is that his or her budget allows for only a brand-new, well-equipped Ford or Chevy. When the sales representative prices the Cadillac, it is simply out of the range the customer can afford. Still, the customer will seldom tell you that. Even if he or she does tell you, it is hard to back out some of the cost without giving the impression that you are gutting the service he or she wanted. Either way you lose.

The way to improve your sales close rate is to find out whether what the customer is telling you that he or she desires actually fits in his or her financial budget. When you do that, your proposal will be exactly on the financial target. The prospect will see you as wiser and more perceptive. Your competitor's proposals might seem nice, but the prospective customer often cannot afford them. There are lots of other lessons, but they will have to be another book.

Machiavelli Would Be Proud

Take Sue—she is really great.

Sue was definitely another learning experience. We hired Sue, and after she was working a month or two, we learned that she really wanted to be a stay-at-home wife. However, her husband wanted her to work. She once had a minor injury and got to stay home for a few days. Then she had another minor accident and then another. Each time her husband would pressure her to go back to work.

You could feel her learning that she needed an injury that would be nebulous enough so a doctor could not really release her to work and her husband would not pressure her to go back to work. If this injury were to happen at work, she would be able to get replacement of her wages. Then her husband would really be happy to have her stay home.

I could see the future, so I hit upon a plan. One of our supervisors would tell a particular competitor what a great employee Sue was and how she was looking for a job closer to her home. Our supervisor made her sound like the greatest possible catch. The competitor took the bait and offered her a job.

Sue liked our company and didn't want to quit. She told me about the competitor's offer and asked what she should do. I talked about the advantages of less travel time, etc., but she liked working for our company. Finally, I had to speculate that the location where she was working presently could possibly be cutting back work in a couple of months. That did it; Sue took the competitor's job, and we gave our problem away. Sure enough, it was not long until she had a permanent workers' compensation claim.

At first, I was rather pleased at how clever I had been. Machiavelli would have been proud. Later, I felt bad about tricking a competitor into burdening itself with a real problem. I never did that again!

A Learning Experience for Kids

As valuable as any college course.

As my oldest daughter, Jennifer, was getting ready to go off to college, we came up with a plan to make her a supervisor for our business near Erie, Pennsylvania. We had two retail customers in the area, and our nearest supervisor was two and a half hours away. One of the store managers didn't like our supervisor, so some changes were going to be necessary anyway. If Jennifer was a supervisor, I could give her a car, an expense account, and a salary, with all of that being a business expense. She would learn about the business and sharpen skills that would be useful in later life. It seemed like a real winner of an idea.

Because retail stores include some very significant floor care work, I put her to work the summer before college with one of our special service teams, performing heavy-duty periodic floor care work. This involved stripping and refinishing or scrubbing and recoating floors. They used large battery-powered automatic scrubbing machines, propane-powered polishers, very large and heavy propane-powered stripping machines, and some of the more traditional electric plug-in machines.

The normal shift was ten hours per night, four nights a week. After the first week, all Jennifer could say was "Dad, that is really hard work. I mean really, really hard. You have to pay these people more." It was an eye-opener for a new high school graduate. I would like to think that such lessons help the transition from high school to the working world.

Jennifer learned her lessons well and soon was off to college. She impressed the other girls in her freshman dorm when she put on her business suit, with shoulder briefcase, and took off to meet a customer, check the quality of work, or just talk to employees. I am sure the car, a full expense account, and a paycheck also helped.

After a month or two on the job, she had to replace someone who was moving out of the area. Jennifer held interviews and followed the company's point-rating system used to help evaluate prospective employees. Part of the process included a thorough background check, which also included a criminal record check.

One charming interviewee seemed so nice. When she reviewed the release for a criminal record check portion of our forms, he confidently assured her he was as clean as a whistle.

She went on and interviewed a number of others. As she was closing up, the charming individual came back to her desk and asked her to sign his paper, showing he was at the interview. As she was signing it, she realized it was a prison release to go to an interview. The guy was doing time. He was in the pokey! When she questioned him about the inconsistency, he had more excuses than a kid caught with his hand in a cookie jar.

Jennifer called me an hour later. She was astonished that someone who was so pleasant and so charming could have been such an incredibly believable liar. That is a lesson I would gladly pay to teach any of my kids. Actually, I did pay for it, and it was worth every penny.

Jennifer was a good supervisor, helping employees learn their jobs and perform better. She knew that pleasing the customer's management was an important part of her job.

She learned quickly and brought some of her natural interpersonal skills into play when she took some of her college girlfriends to Mr. H's store to show them the store and tell them what a really great manager Mr. H was. The manager had one son just a few years younger than the three girls, and he had no daughters. After introducing her two friends, Jennifer told them about some of the things Mr. H did in his store that he was proud of doing. She knew how to flatter, and her cute girlfriends didn't hurt either. Mr. H sucked up the flattery faster than a Hoover Deluxe (industry joke). The job provided interesting training that surely was as valuable as any of her college courses.

Mafia

The money was never recovered, and the crime was never solved.

One day the state police called and asked that I come to a building that we had just secured as a new customer about sixty days before. There had been a robbery sometime before it opened in the morning. Our two cleaning people were possibly the last authorized individuals in the building the night before.

The people in this company had the looks, the vocabulary, and a demeanor straight from the *Godfather* movies. Now, review the next group of circumstances and see what jumps into your mind.

It seemed that the robbers used a crowbar to pry open a rear shop office door that did not have a security alarm. Once in the shop office, they could get to a control box to secure the alarms to the main shop area. In the main shop, they picked up an acetylene torch before going to the administrative office section. They turned off a hidden second security alarm system for the office section of the building. They then pried open two more security doors before going to the second-floor presidential suite.

The presidential suite was something to behold. It had a huge polished black desk, polished black cabinets, and white marble floors and marble statues (mostly nudes). There was polished silver trim all around the room, and three walls were covered with tapestries. Behind one of those tapestries was a hidden wall safe, which had been cut open with the acetylene torch from the shop area. All the smoke alarms in this area that were not part of the hardwired master security system had the batteries removed. The company president reported that four hundred and fifty thousand dollars in cash was taken from the safe.

The company president was insisting that the state police detective immediately question the cleaning people. "It must have been the cleaning people," he kept saying. "They have the codes and the keys." The detective asked whether I could get the people back to the building for questioning but quietly said, "I have to question them, but I have never found the cleaning people to be involved."

I arranged for the two people to come in and speak with the detective. They knew less than I knew, and I didn't know anything. None of us had the faintest idea that there was a wall safe behind one of the tapestries, and none of us had the security code to turn off the shop alarms at the point of entry.

I hope you have this caper figured out. Most of us were sure it was an inside job and there never was any money in the safe. The insurance company paid up because it couldn't prove the burglary wasn't real, and then it canceled the policy at the first opportunity. The money was never recovered, and the crime was never solved.

I canceled our service contract as quickly and as politely as I could. I did not trust this group of people, but I sure did not want to get them upset. I just wanted to get away from any connection with them.

This ex-customer was certainly interesting. A few years later, the top two officials were arrested and convicted of criminal activities not related to this robbery. While they were in jail, an embezzlement probe resulted in the original company closing down. These were the kind of people we were glad to be away from.

Quality versus Luxury

Moving from supplier to partner.

Defining "quality" can be difficult. For most of us, the first thought is to equate quality with price. If we think of cars, perhaps we would equate an expensive Jaguar or Mercedes with quality and relegate a Ford or Chevy to a lower level.

In the business world, we need to change the concept that expense equals quality and recognize that quality is simply *conformance to specifications*. If the expensive car is in the service department garage two days a week, then it is not a quality car, no matter what the cost. If that lower-cost car worked perfectly as designed and never needed repairs for a defect or a failure to operate as designed, then that car had quality.

Recognizing that simple distinction is imperative for a successful business. It prevents you from wasting time and resources on things that are not important. If you set up a system that measures deviation from the specifications, which is really your failure rate, you have the start of a quality system for your company. It should be obvious that you also have to correct any failures at once.

Couple the above measurement with record keeping and feedback to the people doing the work, who can correct the failures, and you will have a world-class quality program. It really is that simple! The harder part is objectively recognizing your failures and then recording them for everyone to see.

It is especially important that you share that information with your customers. It helps move you from being a simple provider to being a business partner. I know that it is a really scary thought to put in writing for your customers all the ways that you are screwing up. It may seem frightening, but if you are going to be good, you have to do it.

Remember that our company was a janitorial service company and people could easily call to report that their desk was dusty or the restroom floor had spots or there was a spider web in a corner somewhere. Such things could easily be seen as failures on our part, with our customer becoming increasingly unhappy.

Conformance to specifications became the key to a quality program, especially in our business. If we were not supposed to dust personal desks, then there was no failure to perform. We did exactly what we were supposed to do; we conformed to the specifications. If the restroom floor spots were a result of not mopping the floor as specified, then we failed to conform. If the spots occurred after mopping because someone had an accident later in the day, then we did not fail to conform to the specifications.

We could provide our customers with an honest list of the total number of service calls that explained which of those were failures to conform and which were not. When you can separate a failure from a general complaint, it is surprising how quickly your employee team can rally around, making sure that those failures do not repeat. In just a few months, almost all service calls fall into the category of not being failures to conform to the specifications.

This then opens an amazing door for increasing communication with your customer. The customer can decide to change the specifications or add new services to eliminate some of the service calls. The important part is that you become part of the team to solve difficulties. You become more of a partner with that customer. Our janitorial service company created such a program and did it so well that we won "supplier of the year" from a Fortune 500 company. We made our quality program work so well that our customer asked us to hold training classes with its own service department.

Creating the program was really at the prodding of one of our customer's facility managers. That fellow could be a real pain in the you-know-where, but we took his basic quality concept and grew it into the program that it became. I owe Joe a vote of thanks.

Quality is not really that hard to achieve, and it has nothing to do with luxury or expense. In fact, a good quality program really reduces expenses. I can prove it or set up such a program for any reader who pays my consulting fee.

Sometimes It Is Good to Be Naive

I walked through an empty building and wondered what that was all about.

After about three years in business, we had a number of contracts in the range of one to five thousand dollars per month in gross revenue. We then made a big jump to a twenty-four-thousand-dollar-per-month contract. This was an important customer. The customer was rather demanding (and I thought really unreasonable in some respects). But we were doing well and getting everything done, including the things I believed were unfair (i.e., doing all the work that was to be done only once a year in the first two months of the contract, without extra pay).

Toward the middle of the second month, my contact at the facility wanted me to come in and see him on a day that the facility was closed for a holiday. I was there! His boss had an office just next to his, and as soon as I was in my contact's office, his boss came into the office and closed the door. A voice in the back of my head said, "Oh, boy, we must have done something seriously wrong."

The conversation was as strange as you can imagine. They both changed the subject several times. They asked questions and more questions. They seemed to be trying to put me in a hot seat, but I had answers for all the questions. The buildings really looked great, and almost everybody knew it, including the top executives. I could even report that all the annual requirements would be completed by the end of the week.

After about thirty minutes, the two looked at each other and made an unpleasant and frustrated look towards each other. They both then looked at me and said something like, "Okay, okay, that's all." Then they actually pointed to the door. I walked through the empty building and out to the parking lot while wondering what that was all about. Then it hit me. I really was naive. They were looking for a bribe or a payoff. I later discovered the previous contractor had sent a regular monthly check to these two.

Sometimes it is good to be naive. I never did pay them. About eight years later, both disappeared. Anyone who knew anything said not a word, and we should all know what that means. I was just sorry it took eight years.

The Truth

Hiring from your competitor.

It seems surprising that some people simply cannot tell the truth. Hank was a permanent part-time employee for our company when his full-time employer closed operations. He asked whether we had more work available, and we moved him into a full-time job. He did well, and our customer thought Hank would make a great supervisor for a number of his smaller buildings. It sounded good to me, and we needed to add more work for this customer, so we created this new job. At first, all seemed to work well.

Later I suspected that Hank had a tendency to stretch the truth, so we had a chat about the need for completely accurate information. Hank admitted that he did have a tendency to embellish a bit but promised to make sure he did not do so in the future.

Slowly I came to realize that Hank didn't just embellish stories; he made up stories. The stories were imaginative, bold, and stupid. As an example, one employee called me and asked when his new car was due to arrive. I had no idea what he was talking about. He explained that Hank told him we were considering him for a major promotion and a car would go with the job. He told me the model number and the particulars of the vehicle Hank told him was coming. The car was several weeks late, and that was why he was calling me. I could not believe that anyone would tell such a stupid lie that would obviously be exposed when the car did not show up. I assumed that this employee must have had a grudge against

Hank and just wanted to get him in trouble. Isn't that what any reasonable person would assume?

A few weeks later, the employee came to my office and asked for some privacy. He then played a phone tape of Hank still promising him a car and providing silly reasons why it was not yet there. Hank had called the employee and started to leave a message when the employee picked up the phone and encouraged Hank to go on and on. I let the employee take the tape because I suspected that after he picked up the phone and did not tell Hank the recorder was still on, it may have been an illegal act.

That day and the next morning, two equally stupid lies were exposed. By 3:00 that afternoon, Hank was given an opportunity to find a job with one of my competitors. That is my euphemistic way of saying he was fired.

However, in this case, he actually did go to one of our competitors, and it hired him at once, thinking of all the inside information he could give. Instead of the competitor gaining inside information, it actually lost business, all because of Hank. Our company got most of that business.

Hank worked for the competitor for about a year and a half before it figured it out and fired him. After a spell, Hank went to work for another competitor, with the same results. There is another business lesson here. That lesson is to *be really careful when you hire from your competitor.*

Because our company was well known as an excellent company, both of our competitors must have thought that they were getting a bargain.

I learned that some people have the capacity for lies so bold, so outrageous, and so stupid as to stagger your imagination. They also do so with such a straight face that you would not believe it possible.

Creative Thinking

Let's go outside the boxes.

There was a large manufacturing plant in a community forty-five minutes from my home, the community where we started the business. I had not yet made a sales call at this place. It was much larger than any customer we had at that stage of growth. The manufacturing plant wanted to hire a contract cleaning company and eliminate the in-house cleaning staff. The union had to resist, and the issue went to arbitration. The company's right to contract the cleaning services was upheld by the arbitrator.

The union had to go through the motions of being upset, but the truth was that few people were really upset. The manufacturing company's employees with the least seniority were bumped back to the cleaning jobs, and they hated it. These employees would have much preferred collecting unemployment compensation.

The manufacturing company sent out an RFP (request for proposal) to every service company it could find. I attended a preliminary meeting with fourteen other companies. Some of those companies were discouraged because of the potential problems with the union, but most intended to respond.

The problem facing our company was how to beat out so many other companies. Some of those companies had been in business long enough to have a great client list and generally a greater credibility than our still very new company. With that many companies, we could not hope to be the low bid, and in that large a field, a low bid would no doubt mean that you were in big trouble. We needed to find a way to be smarter and not lower priced.

The manufacturing company had three shifts per day, seven days per week. The late-night shift and the weekend shifts were normally very light. This was a glass manufacturing plant, and the furnaces could not go cold. Each shift had three cleaning people working eight hours each day. That was a total of nine eight-hour people each day, seven days per week.

I examined the time required to actually perform the required work and found that much less production time was required. The people were on eight-hour shifts because that was the work schedule that the manufacturing plants were used to working. It was also because they were unhappy eight-hour people who had been bumped back into cleaning. The employees doing the cleaning had a hard time looking busy, but no management noticed because they were too busy making glass.

Let's look at the glass manufacturing company's employee traffic flow. The employees working the 7:00 a.m. to 3:00 p.m. shift would begin showing up shortly after 6:00 a.m. They would go to the locker room and change into their grubby work clothes and then go to the large cafeteria area for a cup of coffee, perhaps some breakfast, and a general BS session. Three minutes until 7:00, they would hurry out of the cafeteria, leaving a big mess, and almost race to their workstations to relieve their counterparts. The night-shift worker who was just relieved would go to the locker room and clean up. The work clothes would go in the locker, and he would hurry home. No one stopped at the cafeteria on the way out. The same thing happened at each shift change.

There were also plant supervisor offices, quality control offices, and executive offices that needed cleaning sometime during a twenty-four-hour period.

The opportunity that I saw was to forget duplicating the eight-hour-shift concept and arrange a different schedule. It went like this. Four people (two men and two women) would report at 7:00 a.m. for a three-hour shift. All four would attack the cafeteria at 7:00 and be done by 7:45. The cafeteria looked great when any executives arrived for their basic nine-to-five work schedule.

The two male cleaners would go to the men's locker room, which was almost always completely empty in those forty-five minutes since the shift change. They would begin cleaning and be completed just before 10:00. The locker room would look good all day until the next shift, when the process was repeated.

One of the two ladies would go to the ladies' locker room. This area was much smaller than the men's, and only one was needed. The second lady would clean the supervisors' offices and the quality control offices. Having a second lady available provided emergency coverage in the ladies' shower room in the event of a last-minute sick call.

This whole process was repeated for the next shift, except that two of the four stayed another two hours each to clean the executive offices after 6:00 p.m.

Because the third shift and the weekends were so light, we had two people come in for a three-hour shift to lightly police the areas. The customer was using 504 man-hours of labor per week, and we were going to use 206 man-hours of labor per week. I added a full-time site supervisor to my proposal and still was budgeting less than half of the customer's labor expenditures.

Our competitors simply duplicated the customer's work schedule, and as a result, their prices were far higher. While the customer liked our lower price, it really liked our approach and thought we would make a good team for future problem solving. We got the contract and still had it twenty-seven years later when I sold the company.

Epilogue

Observations about the nature of people and business.

Many people have found the collection of true stories in this book to be more entertaining than most fiction. There is something special about knowing that these things really happened. From all of the stories, we can glean some lessons about people and about business. Let me highlight some of those lessons that you may find useful as you traverse the road of life.

1. When running a business, keep the reins loose. People do their best when they can get up to full speed.

2. Most people really do wish to do well.

3. Don't be afraid to do something new. Jump in and, if need be, figure it out later. This lesson is for everyone, including both business owners and employees. Far too often opportunity is lost for a failure of action. Remember that as long as you do nothing new, nothing new will happen.

4. Let people help. A one-person show seldom succeeds. The most successful people are the ones who build a team.

5. All people can have great ideas. Get them to use those ideas. An empowerment style of management often accomplishes this very well.

6. Many entrepreneurial CEOs cannot let go. They keep all information and decision making going through them until it overwhelms them. They burn out, and the staff never learns how to make the necessary decisions. The business dies.

7. Secrecy in a company seldom works. Employees imagine the worst. You are well advised to let people know what is happening for all but extremely confidential matters. It keeps down the hearsay and helps build the team concept.

8. Some people drive the business to new levels of excellence, and others simply go along for the ride. A great business finds ways to help the riders work for its competitors while keeping the people who drive the business.

9. Share success.

10. Trust is a powerful motivator for almost all people.

11. All business is about people. Let people tell you what they need and help them get it. It is a simple formula for success that is rewritten every day in the story of our lives.

12. Success in business has much to do with perseverance and constant adjustments. Stay flexible and improve constantly.

13. Luck has very little to do with success. We make our own luck with hard work.

14. Opportunity is everywhere.

15. Government is the greatest impediment to developing a successful business. Reasonable rules and regulations are necessary in any society. However, the examples shown in the "Government Is Here to Help" chapter are far from reasonable and just some examples of the nonsense with which well-intended people harm all of our society.

16. In our lifetime, government agencies such as the Pennsylvania Human Relations Commission will never end. It isn't so much because of discrimination problems but that the agency simply needs to have problems, real or imagined, to keep its funding and jobs.

17. Businesses do not pay taxes. They never have and never will. But they do collect lots of money and transfer it to the government, and the cost of doing so is included in the product or service. It is so sad that we cannot teach that simple truth in our schools.

About the Author

- Graduate of the University of Maryland, 1965—BS Chemistry

- Served as a Naval Engineering Officer, 1966–1969

- Joined ARA Services in 1970, starting a new division to provide facilities management services to hospitals and colleges. Established an industrial engineering department within ARA to develop and refine the standards necessary for proper cost management of those facilities. As the division grew, Strobel became the regional director of all operations in the Midwest and Mountain states.

- Vice president and director of operations for Corporate Cleaning in Indianapolis, Indiana, 1972–1973

- Founder of Quality Building Services Inc., Greensburg, Pennsylvania, 1973. The company grew to include operations in three states, employing five hundred people when the company was sold in 2004.

- Presently works in the merger and acquisition business for GPA in Hilton Head Island while helping businesses analyze and improve their operations and helping buyers and sellers reach reasonable agreements.

- Presently owns and operates commercial real estate in Greensburg, Pennsylvania.

- Served as a director and officer of his international trade association, director and division chairman for the local chamber of commerce, director and officer of the State Chamber of Business and Industry. Past chairman of the State Unemployment Compensation Tax Committee (a major author of the last two bills) and past chairman of the State Chamber Workers' Compensation Committee. Served as past chairman for the Industry for Workers' Compensation Reform of Southwestern Pennsylvania and the state's Small Business Committee.

- In the community, served as a Scoutmaster and presently serves on the Westmoreland-Fayette executive board as vice president of administration. Served or presently serving as treasurer or president of a local pool club and civic association. Past volunteer high school economics instructor . and past Rotary Club president. Has served on the advisory board of the rehabilitation center in Johnston.

For orders or additional information go to www.fromthejanitor.com